KARL'S KINGDOM

BOOK 2: RISE OF THE DEATHBRINGER PLUS RAGNUS ORIGIN STORY

MARK BOUTROS

Wonderful cover art by Ivan via Miblart
Edited by Jay Brown
Proofread by Nick Hodgson at Root and Branch Editing

Print ISBN: 978-1-9162974-8-7

 Formatted with Vellum

ABOUT THE AUTHOR

Mark Boutros is an International Emmy nominated and PAGE
International award-winning writer who has written for Disney,
the Cartoon Network, Sky One, the BBC and Sky Arts

He was born in London and still dreams of leaving it for a
mountain where he can grow his own food and not be asked to
do things

If you want to know more about Mark visit
www.mark-boutros.com

Instagram: @markboutroswrites
Facebook: www.facebook.com/MarkBoutrosWrites
Not on X or Threads. Too much misery

CONTENTS

1. The Untortured   1
2. Unanswered Questions   10
3. Reunited   13
4. Dragon's Dinner   15
5. Shared Experiences   19
6. Memories   21
7. The Gift   28
8. A Second Chance   35
9. Welcome Back   43
10. For The People   46
11. Buried Alive   49
12. Back From The Dead   51
13. A Friend For Life   54
14. Settling Dust   59
15. Unconditional Love   61
16. Teamwork   66
17. An Unwanted Reunion   71
18. Babysitting   74
19. Sand, Sea and Screams   78
20. A Frenemy In Need   81
21. Tongue Tied   86
22. Secret's Out   89
23. Lord of the Land   96
24. Something Fishy   99
25. Ghost Town   107
26. Feeding Time   111
27. An Unwelcoming Host   114
28. Into the Unknown   118
29. Blue Blues   121
30. A World of its Own   129
31. Sea, Sea, See   134
32. Free the People   137
33. A Helping Hand   140

34. Steely Secrets — 143
35. A Worthy Leader — 147
36. Shared Vision — 150
37. Change the World — 154
38. The Wreckage of Failure — 158
39. Letting Go — 162
40. Sibling Prisoner — 165
41. A Short Reunion — 167
42. Homeward — 172
43. Planning Problems — 175
44. Hargon — 177
45. A Deadly Resurrection — 180
46. A New Power — 182
47. Facing Death — 187
48. Unwanted Responsibility — 192
49. A Hope in Hell — 195
50. Hiding in Plain Sight — 198
51. A Crumbling Kingdom — 200
52. Perilous Plan — 203
53. The Hopelessness Scale — 205
54. An Honest Choice — 209
55. One Life — 212
56. New Life in Death — 215
Epilogue — 220

THE RISE OF RAGNUS

1. Welcome Party — 225
2. The Blame Game — 235
3. The Worst Kind of Show — 237
4. The Reward for Kindness — 240
5. The Power of Punishment — 244
6. The Harshest Release — 248
7. Second Chances — 252
8. Permanence — 256
9. Chance of a Lifetime — 259
10. Ragnus — 261

Acknowledgments   265
Thank You   267

This book is dedicated to anyone who feels like they need a dedication today. Well done you, you've earned it.

THE UNTORTURED

The sunset split through the four icy peaks of Mount Brohl and shone on Oaf's tired green face. He placed his cloak on the rim of the rock bath and picked up a tatty book, while his two-year-old twins, Boofa and Quizmal, sat behind him in their matching cloaks.

He ran his finger down the page until he came to a baker's name.

'Hazwald?' Oaf read aloud and then placed the book on the rocks. He rested his elbows on his cloak and stared at the water. Tortured souls packed the bath, their heads the size of his palm. Their little legs kicked their armless bodies around and they splashed and bumped into each other but nothing changed – just as it hadn't earlier when he said the names, 'Limbus', 'Howp' and 'Keplom.' He couldn't remember the last time a name had worked.

Oaf scrunched his eyebrows and turned to his children. 'Wrong again.' His stomach cramped and he realised he'd been guessing names since sunrise.

He wanted to wrap his cloak around himself and fall asleep. He tossed the book onto a growing pile of failed guesses.

'This is boring.' Quizmal scratched his bald head and huffed.

Boofa frowned and pulled on her hair. She looked more like her mother every day, thankfully. Boofa ran to a rock chest and grabbed a book.

'What about this?' Boofa pointed to a word she couldn't read in a book titled *Hastovia's Greatest Inventors*.

Oaf smiled. Boofa always kept his spirits up. He took the book. 'The inventor of bread with those little seeds in it. Sounds harmless enough.' Oaf whispered a name in Boofa's ear.

'Yeastaw?' Boofa called out.

Oaf hoisted her and her brother onto the edge of the rock bath so they could look in.

Nothing happened.

Quizmal reached his hand into the water and scooped up a tortured soul. 'Do you remember who you are?' he asked.

It blinked, spat on his hand, and jumped back into the fountain.

'Ergh!' Quizmal moaned.

Oaf and Boofa chuckled.

'They do start to remember small things over time,' Oaf said. 'We'll ask again tomorrow.'

Creaking wooden wheels diverted Oaf's attention to the village entrance.

A battered cart struggled up the path, obscuring whoever pushed it.

Oaf stood in front of his children. Nobody ever visited.

'Excuse me!' A hooded man in worn black armour limped out from behind the cart. 'Is this Inquiso Village?'

Oaf nodded to the rock sign next to the man's head: *"This is Inquiso, all nice beings welcome."* 'Yes. And you are?'

'Tired.' The man coughed. A blob of spittle settled on his cracked lips and he massaged his right knee. The sunlight shone against his time-worn eyes and skin. He must have been as old as the rocks of Mount Brohl.

The man approached Oaf. 'Been dragging this cart of books and things around for eight sunsets looking for these icy peaks.' He pulled a rag from his trousers, unfurled it and showed Oaf several squiggly lines and curved, unfamiliar text. 'See, the map they drew is a bit off, so I kept taking wrong turns.'

Oaf nodded, pretending he had any idea about what was going on.

The man wiped his nose on his sleeve. 'You really should get signs to make it easier for people to find this place.'

Oaf gestured to the icy peaks. 'It's an icy mountain. The only one in south Flowfornia.'

The man coughed. 'Well, I'd sooner trust a map than my old eyes. Anyway, I need to see Questions or Oaf.'

'I'm Oaf. Questions has gone to get fruit.'

'Hmm.' The man pulled his hood back and raised a bushy eyebrow. 'Let me check.' He took another scrunched-up rag from his trousers and held it up to Oaf's face. A drawing of a fat circular creature with eyes didn't resemble anything. 'There's a description. Oaf should be taller than the average being, with brown eyes.' He looked Oaf over. 'Yep. He should have a muscular, tough, grass-green frame.' The man squeezed Oaf's arm. 'Hmm, very tough. You must eat well.'

Oaf pulled his arm free from the man's oily grip.

The visitor scanned his rag further. 'Oaf should be the last of his kind. Is that true?'

Oaf nodded. 'Last of the Oafs, but my children are half Oaf, half Inquiso, so that information needs changing.'

'Mmm hmm,' the man acknowledged. 'Last check. Oaf can sculpt anything out of rock?' The man stared at the rag. 'What?'

Oaf picked up a rock and sculpted a tiny, pointy hat. He handed it to the man. 'This place used to be a snowy wasteland because the icy winds killed the Inquisos. But the rock huts I sculpted have given the place a chance again.'

'Well, thank you.' The man placed the hat in his pocket. 'You seem legitimate, so here are a load of books and tortured souls from the Rux Cay across the southern sea.'

Oaf had no idea where or what that was, but accepted the items. 'Thank you.' This was the first batch from across the sea.

'While I'm here, do you mind if I use a toilet bucket?'

Oaf pointed him towards one of the twelve rock huts along the cliff edge. 'All yours.'

'You seem lovely, you know. It's a shame there aren't more of your people.'

Oaf smiled and the man went to do whatever needed doing.

Oaf turned back to his children. 'Right, two more guesses, then we'll pick a story from these books and get you to bed.'

He grabbed two books from a rock chest and handed them over. 'Boofa, you get *Popular Hastovian Singers*, and Quizmal, *Potentially Interesting Families*. Pick a page.' Oaf yawned.

Boofa flicked through the pages. 'This one of her.' She handed Oaf the book – a sketch of a woman with long hair weaved around her body like clothing.

'Okay, she's someone whose singing voice gives people dreams where they can see their future. Do you like the sound of her?'

'Yes!'

'Her name is…' Oaf whispered in Boofa's ear.

'Maarmobo!' Boofa shouted into the bath.

They waited. Nothing.

Boofa sighed.

Quizmal opened his book. 'Erm, this one.' He pointed to a sketch of a small, boring-looking man holding potion bottles.

Oaf took the book. 'The greatest alchemist to ever live.' But several pages had been ripped out. Oaf scratched his chin, wondering if it was too risky. 'Okay, well, Marlens is an alchemist and she's nice, so I guess this man could be nice too. Are you happy?'

'Happy,' Quizmal replied.

Oaf whispered in his ear.

Quizmal clenched a fist. 'Pagar!'

They waited. 'Pagar!' Quizmal repeated, but nothing happened.

Oaf huffed. 'Sorry. Guess that's it for today.'

Quizmal leapt up and down. 'Jimble, Durek, Landell, Grimlaw, Pestil, Bey—'

'No!' Oaf covered Quizmal's mouth. 'You can't just say names, Quizmal.' He waited until his son settled before removing his hand. 'We need to make sure the names we say are of good beings. We don't want to revive evil.'

'But this takes forever.'

Oaf spoke softly. 'We have to be careful. Repeat the rules.'

Quizmal tutted and huffed. He said with no enthusiasm, 'Rule one: No saying names around the fountain without Ma or Pa. Rule two: Only say names that have been selected from books. Rule three: Always ask Ma and Pa before saying a name in case it's on the Board of the Bad.'

'Perfect.' Oaf turned to the Board of the Bad, surprised there were so many names on it, a mix of thieves, warlords and conjurers.

The hooded man re-emerged carrying an over-flowing toilet bucket. 'Where do I empty this?' Bits of waste fell and splatted against the floor.

Boofa and Quizmal stepped away.

'There's a rock tube behind you,' Oaf said.

'Ah, wonderful.' The man poured the waste down the tube and placed the bucket on the ground. 'How do people become those weird little things?'

'They were tortured horribly, mostly by the Man-Hawk, Arazod, and Lord Ragnus. When people have too much inner strength to die from torture, that energy collides with the pain of near death and they turn into these soul puffs instead.' Oaf smiled.

'Well, good luck reviving them.'

'Thanks,' Oaf said. 'You can stay for food if you like?'

The man scratched his nose. 'No, no. But thank you. I've a tavern to go and find. I'm due a drink or ten.' He bid farewell and pushed his cart down the mountain slope.

Oaf turned to his son. 'Sorry I yelled at you.'

Quizmal nodded and hugged him.

Oaf rubbed Quizmal's head. 'Time to get ready for bed. Your Ma should be back soon.'

Later that night the wind howled outside their stone hut. Oaf sat on a stone rocking chair, next to Quizmal and Boofa's beds. The children wore their matching sleeping cloaks and sifted through the sack of dusty books.

Oaf rubbed his eyes. All that reading to find names drained him. Nothing compelled him to read another book, but his children loved stories and he couldn't let them down, especially as he hadn't given them much attention. Was he a bad father for trying to help tortured souls instead of playing with them? He had seen so much pain in the world that he wanted to put a bit of hope back into it. Maybe it would encourage his children to help others too.

Quizmal handed him a book. 'We like the cover of this one.'

Oaf turned it in his hand. The cover was some sort of animal skin and someone had scratched an image into the cover. It was a Man-Hawk holding a lance. Oaf's neck tensed. The creature reminded him of Arazod. 'Can we choose another?'

Quizmal climbed back onto his bed. 'Please. It looks fun.'

The joy in Quizmal's eyes defeated Oaf. 'Fine. But I'll only read a little bit.' He lifted Boofa back onto her bed. 'Blankets first.'

They pulled their blankets over themselves.

Oaf opened the book and read. 'I have been—'

'Pa, do a voice,' Boofa requested.

Oaf smiled and remembered Arazod's whiny, nasal voice. 'I have been lucky enough to be a Man-Hawk, the greatest species of creature Hastovia has ever seen.' Oaf shook his head, amused at the inflated opinion.

'And I have served under some of the greatest generals: Supreme Man-Hawk Sarzo—'

'Who's Sarzo?' Boofa asked.

'He was an evil warlord, and one of the reasons that your Ma's people perished. He was destroying the woodland around Brohl, so there was no wood to protect their homes or make fire with.'

'Really?'

Oaf nodded. 'And you know the Fools who live here?'

The children nodded.

'They were cursed to follow his orders, and then those of his equally evil son, Arazod. He commanded them to do bad things until your uncle Karl and us freed them.'

'When will we see uncle Karl?' Quizmal asked.

'We'll visit him soon.' It had been over a year. There were invitations, but time slipped away and there was always an excuse not to go, with the most common excuse being that it was too far.

Oaf yawned. 'Sorry, back to the story.' He cleared his throat and channelled Arazod's whine. 'And I have served under some of the greatest generals: Supreme Man-Hawk Sarzo, and his daughter, Ryza.' Oaf raised an eyebrow. Arazod had a sister?

'Why have you stopped, Pa?' Boofa asked.

Oaf shook his head and continued. 'And his daughter, Ryza, who was by far the best. She had these majestic spikes on top of her wings...'

Quizmal's eyes widened.

'And she saved the Man-Hawks from peril.' Oaf scratched his cheek. 'Ten of us were making a nest, when fifty witches surrounded us. We had no chance, but Ryza used herself as a decoy to lure the witches into a funnel-like path between the mountains and we turned the tide. The witches shot lightning at us, reducing some of us to bone and ash—' Oaf wiped his eyes. 'But Ryza tricked them into firing at a cliff so rocks fell on the witch army. With the numbers tipping in our favour, we dominated, and Ryza came face to face with... with...' Oaf's eyes opened and closed.

'Pa!' Boofa sat up.

'With the Witch... Master... Ulrad.' Oaf's head hung. The muffled complaints of his children faded.

'Pa!' Quizmal shook him.

Oaf lifted his head and looked at his children. 'I'll finish the story in the... morning.'

Boofa tapped Oaf's leg. 'No, now!'

Oaf leaned his head back and allowed the chair to rock. The book fell from his hand and he fell asleep.

Oaf's body shook and his eyes shot open. Boofa pulled his arm and words flew out of her mouth but Oaf couldn't work out what she was talking about. She mentioned the book, play fighting and tortured souls. Then it was a stream of words.

He held her arm. 'Slower, Boofa. What's wrong?' He wiped his eyes and noticed she was crying and shaking.

'Outside Pa. Outside!'

Oaf stepped outside and his heart thumped so hard it could've exploded.

Demonic, spike-winged feathery evil faced him, and had an arm around Quizmal's throat.

Blood ran down Quizmal's leg.

Anger, fear and desperation flooded through Oaf's body. 'Let my boy go!' He ran towards Ryza.

Ryza pecked the top of Quizmal's head and he cried. 'Stop!' Ryza commanded Oaf.

'Please don't hurt him.' Oaf raised his arms and dropped to his knees. 'What do you want?'

'Gold.' Ryza held a claw to Quizmal's neck.

'Yes. I'll give you everything we have,' Oaf said.

Fools poked their heads out of windows. Oaf lifted his hands towards them to make sure they didn't get involved.

'And food, clothes. And err… What else do you have?' Ryza asked.

'We have books.'

'Pah! Give me gold, clothes and some meat.'

Oaf nodded. 'We only have bread and berries.'

'Ugh. Give me whatever food you have.'

'Okay. Just please…' Oaf looked into his son's eyes. 'It's okay, Quizmal, you're going to be okay,' he said to convince himself. He didn't want to leave his son, but he had to get the items.

He ran inside, knocked over a chair, fumbled for bread and dropped it. Every moment was crucial, but he couldn't stop his body from shaking or the tears from falling. He grabbed everything he needed and then returned. He showed Ryza the items and placed them in a sack. 'Here, now please let my boy go.'

'Throw me the sack,' she said.

Oaf tossed the sack at Ryza's feet. 'Now give me my boy, please.'

Ryza grabbed the sack with her free hand. She shot a sinister smile at Oaf that froze his heart.

Quizmal's eyes widened. 'Pa?'

'I think I'll hold on to him for a while.' Ryza wrapped both arms around Quizmal, spread her wings and took off.

'No!' Oaf ran towards them, jumped and grabbed Ryza's leg, but she raked a talon down his right eye, blinding him and breaking free.

'Quizmal!' Oaf ran to the edge of the mountain but knew he'd never catch them. Blood met the tears running down his cheek.

His son disappeared into the distance.

UNANSWERED QUESTIONS

Karl lay in bed with Princess Sabrinia in his arms, her gown wrapped around her. A blue orb of fire on her bedside stool cast a flickering light on her brown hair and kind face.

'Twenty-two years of birth tomorrow.' She looked up at him. Her eyes had a glow that always seemed new. 'Are you excited?' she asked.

'I think so...' He smiled, but ageing made him think of his life and what he wanted. That same feeling had tormented him for two years. He reached for the flask of water on his bedside stool, sat up and drank.

Sabrinia held his hand. 'Are you okay?'

'Yeah. Yeah, you know.'

She sat up. 'I know.' She huffed.

He wished his brain would forget it just once so he could enjoy being in the moment. 'I keep wanting it to be different.' Even now, next to her, she was far away.

'So do I.' She placed her head on his shoulder.

'You're the queen. Can't you change the rules? Or find

someone who can cast a spell to remove Arazod's soul and bind mine?'

She shook her head. 'I wish I could. But that's it. You get one marriage in this life. Not fair really, as it'd be nice to be able to change your mind.'

He chuckled. He was sure she could change the rules if she wanted to. 'I just… When I die, that's it. I'll have to wander wherever lonely souls go on my own while you're tormented in the Realm of the Dead by that idiot.'

She lifted her head. 'I'd gladly switch places.'

'I'm not sure Arazod is my type.' He hated himself for making out he was the victim. 'Do you think he's dead?'

She shrugged. 'I found Arazod unbearable as soon as he spoke, and I doubt the Great Dragon has more patience.'

Karl nodded. 'Do you ever sense him?'

She exhaled. 'I think so. But I'm not sure if it's my mind playing tricks. There are times I think I can smell his feathers, his stale breath and feel his looming, miserable soul, just around.' She gestured to the room. 'I picture his beak twitching, and his feathers standing on end, looking at me in that predatory way he used to.'

Karl swallowed. 'Sorry to bring it up.'

Sabrinia squeezed his hands. 'It's okay. It's not easy for either of us.'

Karl stroked her arm. He wished he could be happy with how things were, but it was in his core like a heavy, cold stone. 'Hey. If he is watching, then why don't we give him something he'll hate looking at?' Karl smiled.

Sabrinia chuckled and pressed her lips against his.

Karl's heart lightened and he held her face, moving his hands behind her ears.

She placed her hands on his, stopping him.

He looked at the sheets.

'Sorry,' she said. 'It's just, now that you've brought him up, it makes me think about everything, and Father. Not really the kind of thoughts that go with this.' She bit her lip.

Karl nodded. 'I know, sorry. It's my fault.'

Sabrinia placed a hand against his cheek. 'I wish it could be different too.'

He was sure it could be if she wanted it to be, but she was always thinking of her people. It was as if she forgot he was part of her life too.

She kissed him on the cheek. 'Let's sleep so we can get up early to celebrate your day of birth.' She threw a rag over the orb of fire and the room fell into darkness.

REUNITED

Ryza stood on the edge of a cliff, her wings poking out of holes in her new robe. In the distance, five tiny islands dotted the southern sea. The Ivory Archipelago. Home. But why weren't the Man-Hawks patrolling the sky? Her last memory was of a muscular being with rock fists twisting her neck. She was certain she had died.

Ryza tried to remember more, but Quizmal's weeping invaded her concentration.

She flew up to the totem she had left him balancing on. 'Stop crying and be quiet.' She threw a berry into her beak, chewed it and then spat it out. 'How do people live off this rubbish?'

'I want to go home,' Quizmal sobbed.

Ryza rolled her shoulders. 'We all want to go home. Just stay there and don't do anything that makes me feel like killing you more than I already do.' She'd gladly kick him off the totem, but he might prove useful. Having another life to threaten to protect her own had served her well in the past.

She flew above him and hovered. She opened her beak, took a deep breath and released a demonic shriek towards the Ivory

Archipelago. The skin under her arm feathers tingled. She'd missed the raw power in that sound.

If they were there, they would answer her call.

She listened, but no sound returned. She released another shriek and waited. She took slow breaths not to miss even the slightest sound. Waves bashed the base of the cliff and a wolf howled, probably telling her to shut her beak.

Where were they? They should be responding.

She flapped her way back down and huffed. What if they'd been wiped out? What if she was the only one who remained? She rested against the totem and feared the worst. She'd have to visit a village and ask for information, putting herself in a position of weakness.

A faint shriek pierced the air and she tensed. But the shriek didn't come from the Ivory Archipelago. She turned around and wondered if she was going mad, but then she heard it again. She opened her wings. The Man-Hawk's call came from the north, from the spiky black rocks of Mount Hastovia.

DRAGON'S DINNER

*A*razod lay on the cold ground inside a circle of rocks – his bed. He stared at the stalactites on the ceiling, wondering if he'd imagined the sound. There were no Man-Hawks left to be shrieking. He'd seen to that, and if there was one, did he want to see them? Maybe he could get them to help him. Then he'd kill them once he was free.

Water dripped onto his feathers. He shuffled to his right but another drop hit him.

He grumbled. Three years in this miserable cave, living as the Great Dragon's plaything. He hadn't seen his reflection in all that time, but his feathers were filthy and he could see his ribs. His bones creaked whenever he moved and the closest thing he had to a bath was when the Great Dragon's dry, bumpy tongue licked him.

Arazod stared at the beast, roughly thirty feet high and about sixty long, black as the darkness he dwelt in and outlined by the faint glow of the night sun creeping into the mountain.

The dragon's spear-pointed teeth tore through the torso of a boar-hippo. The beast was pure power and death, yet all he ever did was eat, sleep and torment Arazod. What a waste.

Arazod thought about the long list of people he hated, but at the top of the list were two: Karl, who wouldn't die even when Arazod kicked him off a cliff, and Sabrinia, who refused to love him. All she had to do was love him and everything would be different.

Arazod sat up and released another demonic shriek, so forceful it hurt his broken wing. He'd take his chances with a Man-Hawk.

'What are you doing?' the dragon asked in a voice more suited to a small child.

'I like the—' Arazod wheezed, '—echo this cave provides.'

'Well, stop it. That noise makes my skin crawl, and you're disturbing my snacking.'

Arazod fixed his eyes on the dragon's scales. He wished he could grow to the dragon's size and sink his talons into the monster's flesh. He'd shred him and relish the warmth of dragon blood soaking his feathers while he ripped out the beast's insides.

Arazod missed having working wings and freedom.

'Are you hungry?' the Great Dragon asked.

'You know the answer.'

The dragon crunched through the boar-hippo's skull. 'I just like hearing you say it. Go on.' He flicked a sheet of boar-hippo skin onto Arazod's head.

'Agh!' Arazod whined and fought to remove the oily skin-blanket. He threw it down, his feathers a mess of grease and blood. 'Of course I'm hungry! I'm starving!' A waft of rotting flesh shot into his nostrils and he retched. He stared at the dragon with the rage reserved for his murder victims.

The Great Dragon laughed. 'You're cute when you're stressed.'

Arazod shuddered. 'I hope you choke—' he wheezed, '—to death on those bones!'

The Great Dragon raised his head from his meal, turned and brought his face closer to Arazod's.

Arazod raised a claw. The tension in his body turned to trembling fear. 'I didn't mean that...'

The dragon breathed on Arazod's face. The warm stench of devoured creatures clung to Arazod's feathers.

He swallowed his vomit.

'Clean my teeth,' the dragon demanded.

Not again. Arazod struggled onto his bony legs. His stomach twisted, desperate for proper food.

The Great Dragon rested his face on the rocky ground, opened his mouth and rolled his dull red tongue out, creating a fleshy path to more misery.

Arazod stepped onto the tongue and pressed his talons down, hoping to cause the dragon any kind of pain. It amazed him how the monster's teeth were the same size as him. That's how insignificant he had become.

The heat suffocated Arazod and served as a reminder that one puff of fire would be enough to cook him.

Arazod spotted some boar-hippo stuck between two lower teeth. He approached and pecked at the meat, dislodging it. He chewed some and forced it down despite his body trying to reject it. He was lucky it was somewhat fresh today. His stomach turned.

Arazod pecked some more meat out of the beast's teeth. 'All clean.' Arazod grimaced.

The dragon exhaled, knocking Arazod down his tongue and back into the circle of rocks.

The monster retracted his tongue. 'I've been thinking. I know I say it a lot, but tomorrow I think I will finally set you on fire.'

Part of Arazod was relieved. Death was preferable to this tedious routine.

'Time to sleep now.' The dragon lay down, closed his eyes and pinned Arazod under his claw.

Arazod stared up at the stalactites. If only one would fall and pierce his head – or, better yet, pierce the dragon's. A giant, sword-shaped rock sticking out of the dragon's skull, squashing an eye, would be a majestic sight.

A shadow moved in the cave entrance, but when Arazod focused there was nothing.

He closed his eyes, but when he reopened them his breath caught in his chest. Was he hallucinating? His sister, Ryza, hovered in the entrance, a haunting smirk on her beak.

She flew over to him. 'Hello, Little Arazod,' she whispered.

He smiled through the terror. 'Sister—'

'Let's get you out of here.' She grimaced at the stench, gathered the bones of the dead creatures and placed them under the dragon's claw, propping it up.

Arazod shuffled free, keeping his eyes on her. How?

Ryza shook her head; a disappointed gesture he had experienced too many times in the past.

Arazod stood. 'It will come looking for me when it wakes up,' he whispered.

'Just grab on,' she replied.

Arazod wrapped his arms around his sister's neck.

She flew them out of the cave.

Arazod glanced back and wondered whether he was safer staying where he was.

SHARED EXPERIENCES

Oaf held Questions. They had been in the centre of Inquiso for a lifetime, frozen in a helpless hug, not bothered by the icy wind.

Fools stood in their doorways, wearing multiple layers of fur and not saying anything, but Oaf appreciated them being there.

'Why did we try to help those stupid tortured souls?' Questions pulled away from Oaf.

'You don't mean that.' He was right; she loved helping.

'Why did you fall asleep?' she asked.

Oaf bit his lip and squeezed her hands. He already felt like a failure, and knowing he had hurt the person he loved the most made it worse. 'I'm going to go and find him.' He would never forget the moment he told her Quizmal had been kidnapped. Emotions burst out of her face.

'Should I go with you?' Questions asked.

He didn't want her endangering herself too. 'You should stay here, in case they send a message.' On his own he didn't have to worry about anyone else's safety, and he didn't care about his life if it meant recovering Quizmal.

'Can I go with you?' She stared into his eyes and clenched her fists. 'Can I help you find who took him? Can I help you bring our son back?' She trembled.

'It's better if I go alone.' He held her arms.

'Do you think I'll get in the way?' she asked.

He took a breath and closed his wounded eye to fight the stinging.

A Fool stepped forward and scratched its grey nose. 'We can keep watch here and look after little Boofa.'

Oaf ignored the Fool.

Another Fool offered Questions a thin blade of black steel. 'It's been only decorative, but it seems it has a use now.'

Oaf stared into Questions' eyes.

She took the blade and marched into their hut. She walked out with Boofa and stopped in front of the doorway. 'Will I be back soon?' she asked Boofa.

Boofa nodded.

Questions kissed Boofa's forehead. 'Do I love you?'

'I love you too.'

Questions disappeared down the path.

'Questions!' Oaf called out.

The image of Oaf's injured son haunted him. His family had been happy and his heart bursting with joy. Now everything drowned in pain and his heart felt as if it was choking itself. It was all his fault.

The Fool put its hand on Oaf's shoulder. 'Go and find your son. And when you need us, we'll be ready.'

Oaf turned to Boofa and squeezed her. 'I love you so much. I'll be back with your brother soon, but until then your Fool uncles will look after you.'

'I love you, Pa.'

Oaf clenched his fists and followed Questions. He would retrieve his son or die trying.

MEMORIES

*T*he siblings sat on the roof of a barn and left Quizmal, rope-bound and gagged, asleep on the hard mud next to a sack.

A farmer, his wife and young child, scratched, pecked and mutilated, lay by a tree.

Arazod ripped meat from the farmer's severed hand.

Ryza pecked shredded human skin out of her talons. 'When I returned to the Rux Cay to finish the new nests, Favron and I were ambushed. Some brute with rock fists bashed Favron's skull until it was unrecognisable. Then he tortured me. The next thing I know I'm naked by a fountain in an icy dump.'

Arazod's heart clenched. He hoped she hadn't seen him that day. Had he known more about tortured souls back then he would've made sure Lord Ragnus crushed her. 'Who was this brute?' Arazod asked.

'I don't know. But he twisted my neck until it started to tear. If they were bandits they would've made it quick, so I can only assume it was a planned attack.'

Arazod pecked the farmer's finger, avoiding eye contact with Ryza.

'What year are we in?' Ryza asked.

'The tenth raven.'

'Nine years! I've been gone nine years!' She took a breath. 'Whoever did this will suffer.'

Arazod scratched his neck feathers. 'And I will help you.'

'Where are the other Man-Hawks? And Father?' Ryza stared at the side of Arazod's head.

He swallowed. 'When nobody found your body, our father heard you were sighted and searched for you—' he wheezed. 'But after years of searching, he met his death.' Arazod scratched his feathers and remembered digging his talons into his father's throat and then shredding it. 'Oh, we mourned. But whoever murdered him made him give them command of the Fools and they attacked our home during his funeral.' Arazod threw the bones away.

Ryza dug her talons into the edge of the roof, a flicker of emotion in her cold eyes. 'We need to make the Man-Hawks great again.' She stood and stretched her spiked wings. 'We're going home.'

Arazod pushed himself up to his feet. His stomach ached and he wasn't sure if it was from his first substantial meal in three years or the thought of going home. 'We shouldn't. It's been long deserted. It might be—' he coughed. 'Dangerous.'

Ryza stared into the distance. 'We're going home.'

Arazod's feathers felt hot. He'd hoped he would never have to return.

Ryza pointed to Quizmal. 'Before we go, kill that idiot. We don't need him anymore.'

Arazod shook his head, scared to oppose his sister, but he wanted to prove his use, and Ryza had told Arazod where she had kidnapped Quizmal from. 'Perhaps we should keep him a while longer,' Arazod suggested.

'No,' Ryza said.

Arazod had no doubt Oaf would come for Quizmal. 'But his

father is the strongest being in Hastovia. The only way to best that strength is by using fear. And Oaf will be searching for his son.'

Ryza nodded. 'Very well, Little Arazod. But he's your responsibility.'

He nodded.

They flew to the Ivory Archipelago and landed on the shore.

Arazod dropped Quizmal onto the sand and left him shivering.

Arazod had long forgotten about his home. Built into the hillside was their abandoned town of ivory, covered in nests and thick twisted webs. Humans had inhabited it before the Man-Hawks took it. Now it was lifeless; a monument of death.

The arch was the large, angry face of the first known Man-Hawk, Cyran, and the entrance was through his beak. A crack ran through one of his stone eyes.

A statue of Supreme Man-Hawk, Sarzo, stood to the left of the arch, while a beheaded statue lay on the ground to the right. The surrounding ruined islands showed no life.

Ryza fanned her wings out. 'What happened here?' She stood over the bones of a fallen Man-Hawk.

'It was brutal,' Arazod said. 'Being back makes the screams of the dead loud again.' He stood exactly where he was when he watched the last Man-Hawk get speared through the back of her head.

Ryza walked through the beak. She kicked some bones and shrieked.

The cry chilled Arazod's feathers. 'We should go, dear sister. There's nothing here for us.'

'Shut up.' She shrieked again and stared into the remains of her home. 'I need to see Father's tomb.'

They walked through the eerie wreckage and down rocky steps to a web-covered stone double door, sculpted in the image of Sarzo's face. It looked so real; the feathered frowning beak and judging eyes. Arazod feared Sarzo would appear from it and peck his head like he used to.

Chains wrapped the door handles, and the shazaq, a split-point steel serrated sword that Arazod had wedged through the handles, was still there.

Ryza ran her claws through the thick webs.

Something shuffled behind them, but when they turned there was nothing.

Arazod reached for the shazaq handle in case Ryza turned on him. 'Okay, well, I'll go ahead and make sure no—'

Ryza pushed him out of the way. 'I'll take that.' She removed the sword, hacked the chains off and pulled the doors open. The smell of rotten corpses and waste exploded out of the tomb.

Arazod covered his mouth. Blood and talon marks covered the inside of the left door. He stood in front of it.

'Speak!' Ryza called into the tomb.

They stepped in and descended, Ryza leading with her sword.

Arazod could kick her down the stairs and trap her inside, but it was too risky.

A streak of sunrise followed them into the depths of the tomb.

Hundreds of Man-Hawk corpses, rotten, atrophied and chained, covered the ground.

'How?' Ryza approached the ivory block their father rested on.

Sarzo's decaying body lay in a burial nest of golden sticks. He held his weapon, the Grave Blade, a two-handed steel sword with small blades welded to its sides. His armour, a crystal cuirass modified for his wings, and a spiked helmet lay at his talons. A thin beam of sunlight shone through a tube from the tomb ceiling, illuminating Sarzo's skull.

Ryza touched the loose skin and decaying feathers on his face. She stroked the wounds on his throat and turned to Arazod.

'Such a tragedy,' he said.

'They're all dead!' Ryza's beak twitched. 'This sort of thing doesn't happen to Man-Hawks! We're stronger than this!'

Arazod put his claw on Ryza's shoulder. 'Let's go. It's too sad here.'

She nodded and they turned away.

'Ryza?' a voice strained from the wall.

Arazod's feathers shook.

'What was that?' Ryza placed the sword by the block and grabbed the Grave Blade. She shrieked.

It couldn't be.

Ryza pressed her head to the tiled wall and walked along it.

'What was what? Your mind must be toying with you?'

'Quiet!'

She shrieked again.

A shriek came from beyond the wall.

Arazod backed towards the steps. A sickness rose in his throat. A nightmare worse than living with the Great Dragon was coming true.

Ryza moved a pile of bones. Underneath, a small tunnel descended into a pit.

Roughly twenty emaciated Man-Hawks, still alive but weak, were huddled together. Their wings, ankles and wrists were chained. They must have tried to dig their way out.

'Arnul.' Ryza pulled Arnul up. He still wore his breastplate and his beak and talons were worn. A scar ran down his cheek.

'My General. You're alive.' He fell to a knee. 'You!' His eyes widened and he hopped towards Arazod.

Ryza grabbed Arnul's arm.

'He fled and left us all to die! We had to eat our brothers and sisters to survive!'

Arazod raised his claws. 'I fled so we could live to fight again. I would have returned sooner but I was captured.'

'I heard you laughing during the battle,' Arnul said.

'No,' Arazod replied. 'It must have been—' he wheezed. 'Whoever committed this atrocity.'

Ryza held Arnul's shoulder. 'Little Arazod did what was right. He would have joined you in here otherwise.'

Arazod lowered his claws. 'It's true.'

Arnul took a deep breath. He turned to Ryza and dropped to his knees. 'You will always have my loyalty.' The other Man-Hawks climbed out of the pit and dropped to their knees.

Arazod wished they respected him the same way. He dropped to his knees.

Ryza cut Arnul's chains and gave him the shazaq. 'Unchain the others.'

Arnul shook his limbs and released his friends.

Ryza threw off her robe, took her father's armour and helmet and put them on. She touched the symbol of the Man-Hawk on her chest. It depicted talons crushing a skull. She flew up the steps.

Arazod watched her, desperate to avoid his victims' eyes.

A spider-frog blocked Ryza's exit. Its big frog eyes and mouth pointed at her, and its eight spider legs pressed against the walls.

'Move,' Ryza commanded, ignoring the fact that it wouldn't understand. She drew the Grave Blade back, ready to strike.

The spider-frog opened its mouth. Instead of a tongue, a long web shot out.

Ryza rolled under the web and it whizzed past Arazod's face. Ryza wedged her sword through the creature's chin and twisted the blade. She pulled the sword out and the creature flopped to the floor. Its blood ran down the steps.

'Feast on this disgusting thing. Then we go!' Ryza shouted into the tomb.

Arazod, along with Ryza and most of the Man-Hawks, washed himself in the sea on the west coast of Flowfornia.

Arazod's previous owner emerged from Mount Hastovia. Even from this far the Great Dragon took up a chunk of the sky.

The beast flew to the top of the mountain then descended and searched the rocky paths.

Ryza stood next to her brother. 'I don't like dragons. Their power bothers me.' She turned to Arnul. 'Any power greater than ours needs to be destroyed.'

He nodded. Six Man-Hawks returned from scouting, carrying nets and spears.

'Good work,' Ryza said.

She turned to Arazod. 'Care to join us gathering boulders, Little Arazod?' She smirked. 'Oh, sorry. I keep forgetting.' She nodded at his broken wing.

The other Man-Hawks chuckled and Arnul smirked. 'Not much use, are you? A Man-Hawk without the hawk bit.'

Arazod wanted to dig his talons into Arnul's eyes but he smiled. Arnul's time would come.

Ryza fanned her wings out. 'We're going to see to it that nothing threatens us ever again. I hate that you have all suffered, but I promise you we will become the most powerful creatures in Hastovia and never suffer again!'

Her Man-Hawks smiled and shrieked.

Arnul held his sword across his chest.

Why were they so ready to die for her but never for him?

'We shall return to the Rux Cay where we were planning to expand our home,' she said. 'From there we will build our base and plan where to attack first.'

Arazod had a better idea. 'Sister. I know a place we can live. A place already plentiful with food and supplies. And a good place to get back into the spirit of battle.'

THE GIFT

*K*arl hooked his stone shield, the Star of Reech, onto the back of his stone armour. He placed his stone helmet on and stared at a hay-stuffed grinning dummy, which sat on a cart by the well in the middle of Flowforn's red-pebbled courtyard.

About a hundred Flowfornians stood in the shadow of the castle towers, watching, waiting.

An arrow pierced the dummy's heart and stuck the figure to the back of the cart.

Karl clapped and cheered along with the rest of the crowd.

Hargon tapped his fist against his scratched copper armour and bowed to his audience. He flicked his red hair over his shoulders. 'Happy day of birth, Karl.'

'Thanks, Hargon. You could've just given me some gold, though.' Karl smiled.

Hargon cast a glance at Bar Witch, whose tunic was dotted with ale stains.

'Lucky shot.' She folded her arms.

Karl and Princess Sabrinia shared a smile. Hargon had changed a lot since the invasion. From a hopeless guard who loved painting, he was now a hopeless guard who loved painting but was also handy with a bow and arrow. Sabrinia had seen to it that everyone trained in some form of weaponry. Karl dreaded war, but at least they would be somewhat prepared if they had to defend themselves.

He placed his hand on the grip of his steel sword, sheathed to his belt. The experiences of three years ago had scarred him more than he knew. It could be a nice and sun-blessed day like today, and then something as small as a bird flying would send his mind racing into scenarios of war. Since they'd defeated Arazod and Lord Ragnus, they had received invitations to battle, which was odd, as it seemed like sport to armies who simply wanted to test their strength. Sabrinia had rejected them, but Karl worried that by training they would be viewed as a threat, as though they were preparing to conquer, when all they trained for was to avoid death.

Sabrinia stepped up to the platform. She tucked her hair under her helmet and put her steel breastplate over her gown.

'I'll give you a tip,' Hargon said. 'It's all in the strength of the holding arm. I lean the bow's lower limb up a bit to get a nice gentle dip.'

She turned to him. 'Thanks. I'll be sure to keep your tip some-where safe.' Sabrinia tapped her arrow against a waste barrel and smiled.

Hargon chuckled and sat on a stool next to Bar Witch, who shuffled away. Hargon lifted a stone slab and paint palette from the ground and placed them on his lap.

Sabrinia picked up her recurve bow named Sastin, after her father. It had a steel grip and limbs made from the bendy trees of Herbis Forest. She exhaled.

The crowd fell silent.

She went through the motions she always told Karl about. She relaxed her posture, positioned the string in the first groove of her first three fingers, raised her bow arm level with the target, and drew the bowstring back to the side of her face. She looked along the arrow, aligned it, and let go.

The arrow pierced the dummy's left eye.

The crowd roared and cheered, 'Sabrinia! Sabrinia!'

She bowed.

'Well done, Princess,' Hargon said.

She approached Karl. 'Not bad, eh?'

'I still don't understand how you've improved so quickly. You must be taking secret lessons.'

'I'm just a natural.' She shrugged. 'Are you enjoying yourself?'

'Yeah. I just wish the others were here.'

Sabrinia held his hand. 'Just because they're not, it doesn't mean they're not thinking of you.'

'You're right.' He sighed. He missed Oaf and Questions. Sure, Questions would be asking him stupid questions, but he wouldn't mind that. He also missed the adventurers. He'd grown used to having Sags wake him up every day to train. At the time he had hated it, but Flowforn was lonelier without him.

'Hey, how about I give you a surprise to distract you?' Sabrinia raised her eyebrows.

Karl grinned. 'Really? Yes please!' She'd never been so forward.

'Peezant!' Sabrinia called out. Her dirt-orange parrot flew through Flowforn Arch.

Karl frowned. 'Being pecked on the head isn't the surprise I was hoping for.'

They entered the arch behind Peezant and Karl's heart lightened.

Marlens beamed, muddy from travel and her steel armour scratched. She carried a sack over her shoulder, grabbed a jar of a red mixture as bright as her hair from her potion belt, tossed it into the air and caught it.

Frong, his beard down to his waist, sheathed his spear onto

the back of his armour and grinned at Karl. He was still as round as ever but the joy of adventure shone in his eyes.

Sags pointed at Karl and smiled. He sharpened one of his throwing axes against his gauntlet and looked more alive than Karl had ever known. Adventuring was what these three lived for, and it showed.

'You knew?' Karl asked Sabrinia and removed his helmet.

She kissed his cheek.

Peezant landed on Karl's shoulder and pecked his ear.

'Go away, Peezant.' Karl waved Peezant away with the back of his hand, so he went and landed on Sabrinia's shoulder.

'Looks like we're just in time.' Marlens hugged Karl. 'We've got a proper nice present for ya, old pal.'

'Less of the old,' Karl said.

Sags grunted.

'I missed you too, Sags.' Karl squeezed him. 'I know I always complain about you waking me up to train, but can you please wake me up every day from now on?'

Sags grunted and patted him on the back.

Karl released the hug. 'And be warned, I've been practising. I can definitely take you now.'

Sags grunted.

Karl turned to Frong. 'I still don't understand all of his grunts, but that one was rude, wasn't it?'

Frong nodded. 'But not without truth.'

'It's so good to have you all back!' Karl said.

Frong grabbed Karl's shoulder. 'We actually got back to shore a few sunsets ago, but thought it would be better to appear for a special occasion. More dramatic.'

'We've got something to show ya.' Marlens placed the sack on the floor and removed a jar containing a flapping blue-spotted red hair with a green root. It was as thick as a wrist.

'Well, that's disgusting.' Karl grimaced. 'What does it do?'

The hair slapped against the glass, leaving a slimy residue.

Marlens held the jar closer to Karl's face and he backed away. 'This magical relic is the back hair of the wizard-lizard.' She grinned.

Frong continued the story. 'We found it in the Crystal Mines of Erebost, on an island three days off the coast of West Flowfornia. We pinched the hair while the creature slept. It wasn't happy, but we managed to escape with only a few cuts and burn marks.' Frong showed Karl his scarred elbow and a patch where he once had hair.

'Okay, but what does it *do?*'

Sags grabbed Karl's chin and made him face him. 'I'll tell you,' he said in a gruff voice.

Karl jumped back. 'You speak! He's speaking! You have a voice. Is this a trick?' Karl's skin tingled.

The others laughed.

'You all know?' he said.

Sabrinia stroked his arm. 'It was the hardest secret I've ever had to keep.'

'How's this happening?' Karl stared at Sags.

Sags took the jar. 'You pull a piece of the hair off, stick it to whatever you've lost, and it grows back! Only problem is it grows back that colour so I look like I've licked some sort of weird berry.' Sags stuck his tongue out, half normal and half red with blue spots. 'The hair itself grows back, so you can use it forever!' He handed the jar back to Marlens.

She returned it to the sack. 'We wanna study it and use it to help improve healin' in Flowforn and then more of Hastovia.'

'This is amazing,' Karl said, giddy. 'Say something else. Anything.'

Sags shrugged. 'Erm… door.'

Karl's mouth fell open. 'Wow.' It didn't seem real.

Frong laughed. 'It doesn't really work for small cuts and things, but if you lose a limb…'

Karl welled up. 'This is the best birthday present I've ever had.'

Marlens chuckled.

'What?' Karl asked.

Frong smiled. 'That's not your present.'

'Yeah. Follow us.' Marlens walked towards the tavern.

'Hold on,' Sags said.

Marlens stopped.

'Today seems like a day of great celebration. So…' Sags took Frong's hands and looked into his eyes. 'Frong, thank you for always sticking by me, even when I could only communicate with grunts.'

Frong shrugged. 'Well, I had nowhere else to go, no other friends, and you're the keeper of the gold in this coupling.'

Sags chuckled and nodded. 'We've had some incredible adventures. We've seen mountains, seas, forests, beasts, relics and tribes.'

Sabrinia squeezed Karl's hand.

Frong raised a finger. 'And we've consumed many a delicious beverage in the tavern.'

'That too.' Sags released Frong's hands and pulled a necklace of different coloured pebbles from his pocket.

Marlens grinned and placed a hand on her chest.

Sags dropped to both knees. 'I'll never tire of your stories, and I'll never ask you to cut your beard.' He held the necklace up. 'These pebbles are from different adventures we've had over thousands of sunsets. Are you ready to go on a new one?'

Frong raised his hands to his mouth. 'Sags… Wha… Do you?'

Karl wished he and Sabrinia could have this moment. He'd planned to propose by giving her a book with drawings of all the monsters they had come up with playing three-word monster. The drawings were awful, but the love he had put into the book would have made Sabrinia happy. He swallowed the disappointment that the book would remain in a crate.

Frong dropped to his knees and bent his head forward. He dabbed his beard against his eyes.

Sags placed the necklace around Frong's neck, pulled his beard through it and they embraced.

'I can't believe it,' Frong said.

Sabrinia smiled at Karl. 'I'll ask the bakers to make a special meal.' She walked away.

Karl watched her. The happiness of the moment was dampened with regret that he couldn't stop her marrying Arazod. If only he had arrived faster. He shook the thought out of his mind. This was Frong and Sags' moment to celebrate. 'I didn't think this day could get any better,' Karl said.

Marlens put a hand on his shoulder. 'We'll see about that.'

A SECOND CHANCE

Karl walked through the wooden door of the Adventurer Tavern, where Bar Witch sprinkled spices into a barrel of ale.

Arazod's old axe, the Soul Bleeder, hung on the wall behind the bar.

Karl scratched his cheek and held his helmet. 'Sags, you know, I always imagined your voice would be more…echoey. Like a powerful being.'

'Sorry to disappoint you.' He cleared his throat and in a deep voice said, 'How about this?'

The hairs on Karl's neck stood on end and he laughed. 'Speak however you want. This is just amazing.'

Frong dipped a flask into one of the barrels and drank the brown contents. 'Delicious,' he told Bar Witch. He took an old leather-bound book from a shelf by the fire.

Marlens led Karl to a back room full of barrels.

Karl smiled. 'Are we going to the secret room? I love the secret room.'

'You know it.' Marlens took a blindfold from a shelf.

'Can my present be that you let me see how you get in?' Karl asked.

'Sorry, Karl,' Frong said. 'Information is dangerous, and a room that will one day be full of magic relics is attractive to evil-doers. If you don't know how to get in, you're less likely to get tortured for the knowledge.'

The thought that someone would torture anyone else reminded Karl that evil would always exist. 'I get it.'

Marlens tied the blindfold over Karl's eyes.

'You see,' Frong said. 'The primary reason for torture is not pleasure, but to find out information. It all started with a queen in Hazmash, a castle north of Flowfornia, two hundred and forty sunsets by boat—'

'Please, it's my day of birth. I know it's been a while, but can we avoid the stories just for today?'

'Okay, I'll tell you the rest tomorrow. Perhaps I'll remember more of it,' Frong said.

Barrels rolled and stone scraped. Something clicked and a door opened. Strong hands gripped Karl's shoulders and ushered him forwards.

A faint green glow flooded the blindfold. 'What's going on?' His face warmed.

Sags lifted the blindfold from Karl's face.

A glowing green orb dazzled Karl's eyes. He squinted. 'Is that orb some kind of food?'

Frong patted him on the back. 'It would be a waste to eat it.'

'We agreed no stories until tomorrow.' Karl detected Frong was about to launch into one.

'This one is worth listening to.' Sags removed his armour and placed it against the wall.

Frong took the relic. The green glowed against his beard, giving him a mystical aura. 'This is not a normal relic, Karl. This is a god in a relic.'

Karl blinked, not sure what anything meant.

'Maybe you should sit, Karl.' Marlens placed the jar containing the hair of the wizard-lizard on one of the empty plinths lining the stone walls, then grabbed a stool from next to the entrance.

Karl sat and faced Frong, who opened the book. 'When the world began, it was just Mother Hastovia. While it is more favourable today to believe the world is just flat land—'

'Because it is,' Karl said.

'Well, in the past we believed the world was her without doubt.' Frong showed Karl a page with a sketching of a map. The central islands and oceans formed the body of a woman with her arms stretched above her head. 'Where we are is somewhere on the right knee.' Frong placed his finger over the location. 'Tens of thousands of sunsets to the north, the land of mountains is the chest area. Then there's a canyon that is the neck, before you get to a large pit, a couple of caves that go underground into her nostrils, and craters that make up her eyes. Her energy is what created the eight gods.'

'And the relic?' Karl asked.

'Patience.' Frong scratched his beard and turned the page to a drawing of a muscular woman rising from the waves. 'You had Octorion. She was born of the force of the thrashing waves and her role was to feed nature. She was as gentle as the sea settling on the shore, but also as brutal as a typhoon.'

'Okay...' Karl still didn't understand the relic.

Frong turned the page to a drawing of a tall woman wrapped in twigs that snaked around her body. 'Naturais was formed by the breath of trees, and she created the Heart of Hastovia you saw in Lake Shizneh. There are smaller trees of this kind on other islands, tasked with feeding trees around the world, allowing the beauty of Mother Hastovia to flourish.'

Frong turned another page to a drawing of a winged wolf, who didn't have the look of a friendly god. 'There was Shardur,

the youngest and the keeper of darkness, born from the underground from the dirt and decay.'

'Seems she got the short straw.'

'She was the god of shadow and darkness.' Frong cleared his
throat. 'And we live in a world of balance and opposites, so where
there is darkness, there must be light.' He held the orb to Karl's
face.

Karl moved his head back, fearful of the hot energy radiating
from the orb.

'This is Illuminus.' Frong turned the page to the drawing of a
woman sat atop a mountain. She was the most human, bathed in
light. 'She was the god of light. She formed at the highest point in
Hastovia, on Mount Lamors, believed to be Mother Hastovia's
nose, where the sun creates the most warmth.'

'Why's she in an orb?'

'We'll get there.' Frong handed the orb to Marlens.

'Please! This is like listening to someone explain a really
boring dream.'

'Patience, Karl.'

Karl shook his head and looked at Sags, who chuckled.

Frong turned the page to another drawing – an angry-looking
horned man made of fire, riding the wind. 'You had Pyralus, the
god of wind and flame. When wind got caught in a volcano, it
caused chaos in the heat and from the violence he erupted into
birth. They say when the wind howls, that's him crying.'

'Why is he crying?'

'We'll get to that.'

Karl huffed. 'Why won't you answer any of the questions
about interesting bits?'

'There is a specific order of events.'

Karl folded his arms. 'It's a boring order.'

'There was Eratul, who emerged from stone and storm when
lightning destroyed Mount Forgul.' Frong turned the page to a
drawing of a woman made of stone, stood at the base of a ruined

mountain holding a flail that crackled with lightning. 'She created the rune stones and formed new mountains to balance the weather.'

Karl tapped his feet against the ground.

Frong turned the page to text. 'There is a god nobody ever saw, but they claim to have heard. These are the stories of people stricken by her words.'

Karl studied the text. It was a mess of words and scratched letters that made no sense.

'They call her Deranga, for people were never the same after they heard her voice. There is no story of where she came from and she never appeared with the other gods.'

'And finally?'

'Finally, there was Death.' Frong turned the page to a drawing of a wraith wearing a tatty cloak. His scythe-like nails resembled blades and where there should have been eyes there was only darkness.

Karl shuddered. 'He doesn't look like much fun.'

'He was born from a combination of light and dark energy. His job was the most important. Energetic harmony. He existed within the realms of life and death, and when there was a build-up of negative energy he would collect it in his eyes and cloak and then release it into the Realm of the Dead. He would also help lost souls to find each other.'

'He should work on his appearance if he wants to avoid being judged as scary.'

'He and Illuminus were in love, which made some of the others jealous.' Frong closed the book, *The Godly Godsfolk: Third Edition*. 'If you ever want to read more on each god, you can borrow this.'

Karl smiled. 'I think I'll pass. Why's it edition three?'

'You know. Stories change. New learnings happen. Before it was ten gods.' Frong chuckled.

Karl sighed. 'So the relic?'

'Yes. The gods created people and creatures as a gift to Mother Hastovia. They worked together to do so, and their creations roamed Hastovia with them. It was great until the numbers grew.' Frong stroked his beard. 'The gods told people not to overdo it with the reproducing, but they didn't listen. It was often hot, and they lacked restraint. There are only so many games you can play with rocks and sticks before reproducing becomes the preferred leisure activity.' Frong chuckled. 'It meant the gods had less time to spend with everyone. If someone needed help at the same time as another, the gods would be over-stretched and someone would be let down. To help, they created relics, as you've seen. Items to assist for whatever they were in need of.'

'You're still not telling me about this particular relic.'

'Relax. It's not about the destination, it's about the journey there.'

'I'll die of old age before this journey's over,' Karl said.

'So, power corrupts. And some people used their new power to harm. Octorion, Eratul and Pyralus had enough and punished those who did wrong, but they went too far. Death caught them slaughtering a village, so he battered Eratul as a warning. The others apologised and swore they would no longer harm people, but they lied. They intimidated Naturais into helping them to capture Illuminus. With the use of Eratul's rune magic, they sealed her in a rune.'

'Why?'

'Because Death was the most powerful, the purest balance of energy. Having no heart and being able to exist in both realms made him invincible. He could appear as a phantom, or cross into the land of the living to attack and then vanish again, so they used his only weakness to make him appear in front of them. Love.'

Marlens handed Karl the orb. Behind muscular fibres was a

green ocean and sandy shore, where a woman sat with her head between her knees.

'They used Illuminus to command Death, saying that if he didn't do as they wished they would destroy the rune with Illuminus in it. So they made him kill people, the beings he loved. It was a massacre.'

Karl shook his head. 'That's horrible.'

Frong nodded. 'It seems they were worse than the corrupted people. However, Naturais felt guilty and secretly loved Death, so she stole the Soul of Illuminus rune. Death thanked her, but when Naturais confessed she did it because she loved him and hoped he would be with her, he killed her for her selfish motives. The other gods found him as his nails shredded her tree-like body, and before Death could take Illuminus, Pyralus grabbed her. They used Illuminus to make him come into the world of the living, where with rune magic and the power of their combined elements, they froze Death. Ending his existence was too merciful, and they wanted him to think and to suffer for eternity.'

'So he's frozen somewhere, just remembering all of this over and over?' A chill shot through Karl's body.

Frong nodded.

'Shardur offered to take the rune into the dark realm and leave Illuminus to suffer forever among the souls of the damned, but she loved Illuminus, so she must have hidden her in our world instead. We found the Soul of Illuminus in an underwater cave. And now is the part of the story you will be interested in.'

'Really? All that for one part?'

'There are many types of rune magic. Among them are complex spells that are used to harm, and sealing spells. Those work by sealing power and turning it into a rune. That rune can then be used, but only once – almost like a farewell to a power. In war, runes would be made from captured warriors and used against the enemy. A final, poetic punishment. Your power used to damn your people.' Frong turned his head. 'Marlens?'

She nodded. 'Illuminus had the main power when it came to creating beings. You know, her light was life and warmth and all that. So this rune – well, it can be used to bring someone back from the dead.'

Karl's eyes widened. 'Are you sure? This isn't like that portal story all over again, Frong?'

Marlens nodded. 'I studied lots on energy and runes. There are stories of Illuminus resurrecting people whose lives were ended by things like murder and sickness. She was the original healer.'

Sags put an arm around Karl. 'You know how you only knew your mother for less than a day?'

Karl's limbs weakened and tears filled his eyes. The image of his mother, Larnela, lying in his arms, her blood seeping through his fingers invaded his mind, as fresh as the day it happened.

'Happy day of birth, Karl,' Sags said.

WELCOME BACK

Karl walked towards the cemetery. He clutched the orb, his chance to mend a wound on his life. His body burned with power – exciting and terrifying. Nobody should have this, but he would get to see his mother. He would get to have a relationship with her and ask her all the questions he never got a chance to. He'd get to hug her.

Sags, Frong and Marlens followed.

'You okay?' Sags asked.

Karl stopped. He looked at the orb and remembered the life draining from his mother's face. It wasn't fair. 'I think I should do this alone.'

'Are you sure?' Sags asked.

Karl nodded. 'Thanks. I just think it would be weird if everyone was there. It might startle her.'

Frong placed a hand on Karl's shoulder. 'Understood.' He raised a finger. 'Just remember. You have to touch the Soul of Illuminus to her chest, on the heart. Or if she's a bag of bones, where the heart would be, which is about here.' He poked his finger into Karl's chest.

Karl appreciated everything they'd done. 'See you soon, with my mother next to me.'

Sags smiled. 'We'll save you both some food.'

'Don't make promises you can't keep,' Marlens said.

Karl smiled. He walked through the alleys, ignoring the usual sounds of people selling food and strange items, until he arrived at the cemetery gate.

'Karl,' Sabrinia called out.

He turned. Her face glowed.

'Where are you going?' she asked.

'I'm just going to visit my mum's grave. I'll join you all in a moment.'

'What's that?' She nodded at the orb.

'This?' She too had lost a loved one. Maybe he should offer it to her. No. It was his. 'It's just a fancy stone I want to lay by her grave. Supposed to bring her peace in the Realm of the Dead.'

Sabrinia nodded. 'Well, I'll see you back in the courtyard?'

'Yeah.' Karl kissed her on the cheek and entered the cemetery.

He stood in front of his mother's blue gravestone, carved with her name – Larnela. He didn't know their family name. 'Hi, Mum. Still feels weird that I didn't get to call you that more.' Karl took a breath, his body numb. 'If this works, we'll be able to get to know each other.' His eyes flooded. He wondered if he should have food and water to offer her straight away in case she didn't want to see other people, but realised none of that mattered. He needed her back first.

Karl stared into the orb. Illuminus had her head in her knees. He wondered if she was in that position when the other gods trapped her.

He was sure her head moved so brought the orb up to his eye. Illuminus shot to her feet and screamed at Karl. He dropped the orb.

Karl picked it up and held it at arm's length.

'Life is death!' she yelled. 'Life is death!'

'Life is death?' Karl repeated. He shrugged and dropped to his knees, placed the orb by Larnela's stone and used his sword to dig into the soil. He didn't care if anyone watched. He uncovered the top of her coffin and stared at it, his mouth dry and his throat aching. He dug his nails into the coffin and pulled at a plank.

A boulder fell out of the sky and crashed next to Larnela's grave. The force knocked Karl onto his back and the orb rolled next to a tree. Karl groaned and held his ribs. What was happening? Another boulder crashed into the tree. A branch fell, covering the orb.

Man-Hawk pairings carrying boulders in nets shrieked through the sky.

Karl stood, picked up his sword and unhooked the Star of Reech from his back straps.

A Man-Hawk landed in front of Karl and pointed her spear. She thrust but Karl deflected it with his shield. The Man-Hawk was fast, but Karl's sword was lighter and his shield gave him an advantage.

The Man-Hawk's stance was too wide.

Each time Karl blocked, the Man-Hawk became more aggressive, compromising technique. Sags had taught Karl to study his opponent while defending.

The Man-Hawk swept the spear at Karl's legs, but Karl jumped and lunged forward, stabbing the Man-Hawk between her shoulder and neck.

It dropped its spear.

Karl pulled his sword out and whacked his shield across the Man-Hawk's head.

Screams came from the courtyard. He had to help, but the orb glowed under the broken tree and cracked boulder. He would resurrect his mother first.

FOR THE PEOPLE

Sabrinia shot an arrow into the sky. 'Everyone take cover!' The arrow pierced a Man-Hawk's neck. It dropped its side of the net and along with the boulder, crashed into Flowforn's outer wall next to the tavern.

Another boulder smashed through the King's Eye bridge, connecting the top of the King's Tower to the Lookout Tower. The broken stone destroyed the roof of the Great Hall.

Sabrinia's heart choked. Everywhere she looked, something was being destroyed or someone crushed. The statue of her father fell. Was this the end of her people?

She fired more arrows, but the Man-Hawks flew so fast they were difficult to hit. 'Retreat to the alleys!' she yelled to those fighting with her.

A flaming boulder crushed a man and set a cart ablaze in front of a door. Screams came from within the home.

Sags tried to push the burning cart but the fire repelled him.

'We need to put it out!' Sabrinia said.

Two Flowfornians threw buckets of water over the fire but it did nothing.

Marlens dropped her sack. 'Cover me.'

Sabrinia launched arrows into the sky while Marlens ran into her workshop.

Sabrinia approached the cart but it was too hot to get close.

Marlens returned and threw a jar of blue powder onto the cart. A watery explosion extinguished the flames and soaked Sabrinia, Frong and Sags.

They pushed the cart away, freeing a mother and her child.

'We need to get them out of here,' Frong said.

A Man-Hawk flew at Sags with her sword pointed forwards. Sags threw an axe at the creature's shoulder and knocked her head first into a wall.

'There.' Marlens pointed to the broken wall by the tavern.

'I'll do it.' Hargon fired arrows into the sky. A Man-Hawk dropped through the roof of a house.

Sags threw another axe at a Man-Hawk. 'Get everyone into the forest and hide among the trees.'

Hargon nodded and led people away.

A Man-Hawk swooped at Frong and slashed with his talons. Frong leaned back, grabbed the Man-Hawk by the leg and swung him into a statue.

The Man-Hawk struggled to his feet and flew away.

Sabrinia's neck tensed. Man-Hawks swooped in a formation like a giant hawk. 'We won't survive this swarm.'

She took aim at four Man-Hawks carrying a flaming boulder towards the King's Tower.

A Man-Hawk knocked Sabrinia to the floor and raised his talons to strike her, but Sags tackled him to the ground.

The Man-Hawk rolled Sags over and pecked his shoulder. The enemy drew his head back to peck Sags' face, but Sabrinia stabbed an arrow through the Man-Hawk's neck. She picked up her bow and another arrow and took aim, but it was too late.

The boulder smashed through sixty feet of stone, sixty feet of memories, and who knew how many people.

Sabrinia's head throbbed. 'My people.' She ran towards the wreckage.

Marlens grabbed her but she tried to shake free. 'My people!' she protested.

Marlens wouldn't release her. 'We need to fall back to the forest. Stay close to the castle walls. Then when it's clear, we make a break for it.'

'You're no good to your people dead,' Sags said.

A Man-Hawk with a scarred cheek swooped down and chopped a Flowfornian's head off as casually as slicing through an apple.

Sabrinia tried to pry Marlens' hands from around her, but her friends were right. Her eyes filled with tears. She turned away from her people and tried to shut out the screams.

BURIED ALIVE

*H*argon, followed by panicked Flowfornians, neared the broken wall.

A boulder crashed in front of the gap and blocked the path to freedom.

Hargon needed a solution before the Man-Hawks spotted them, but he had nothing. His hands trembled but he tried to stay focused for the others.

Peezant hovered above Flowforn Arch and squawked.

'This way,' Hargon told the people and ran for Flowforn Arch, but two Man-Hawks landed in front of it.

'Back,' Hargon told the people. He ducked behind a building, thankful the Man-Hawks hadn't seen him. He looked for Peezant, but the parrot shook its head.

All those Flowfornians. They were going to die because of him. He took a breath, ready to risk himself to distract the Man-Hawks so the people could make a run for it.

'In here.' Bar Witch poked her head out of the tavern door.

'Quick everyone, to Bar Witch,' Hargon said, relieved. He'd been a leader for a moment and that was long enough.

A Man-Hawk with a scarred cheek swooped down and stabbed an old woman in her stomach.

Hargon followed everyone into the tavern. He worried the scarred Man-Hawk would turn his attention to them. 'What do we do?' he asked Bar Witch.

'Follow me.' She ran into the back room and moved barrels onto stones.

'Surrender or slaughter? Your choice,' a voice yelled from the bar area.

Hargon's eyes widened. He peered into the room and saw the scarred Man-Hawk at the tavern entrance.

'Hurry,' Hargon told Bar Witch.

'Don't rush me!' She pushed a stone to open a secret door. 'Everyone in here.'

Everyone entered. 'Hold the door,' Bar Witch told Hargon.

She kicked the barrels off the secret stones and entered.

'You can close it now,' she said.

'Thanks for saving us.' Hargon closed the door.

Bar Witch turned to him. 'Let's hope the others stay alive and come back for us, otherwise this is our coffin.'

BACK FROM THE DEAD

Karl squeezed and strained his arm between broken pieces of boulder, but the orb was out of reach. He stretched his sword at the orb but couldn't get the angle.

'Karl!' Sabrinia called from the cemetery entrance. 'Come on!'

He couldn't leave the orb. 'I'll follow!'

'We have to go now!' She fired an arrow into the sky. A Man-Hawk crashed to the ground.

'Hurry, Karl!' Sags called out. 'We're overrun.'

He shook his head. He'd resurrect Larnela and take her with him.

'Karl!' Sabrinia called.

Another boulder crashed. He almost had the orb.

'Hello, Karl,' a whiny voice said.

Karl turned. Arazod, his mother's murderer, stood next to another Man-Hawk holding a sword so demonic only the most sinister would wield it.

Karl held his sword and shield in front of him, using all of his restraint not to lunge at Arazod. 'I'd hoped the Great Dragon would've eaten you, but I guess it didn't like the taste of misery.'

Karl pointed his sword at Arazod's companion. 'Who are you? His new servant?'

She smirked. 'I'm his big sister, Ryza.'

Karl turned to Arazod. 'During all the fun we had together you never mentioned a sister.'

Ryza's beak twitched.

Karl shook his head. 'And to be honest, he displayed all the characteristics of an only child.'

'Give me the sword,' Arazod said to Ryza. 'Let me end him.' He reached for the sword but Ryza moved it away.

'I think I prefer you,' Karl said to Ryza.

Ryza flew at Karl and swiped her bladed wing at him.

He ducked but she cut his cheek.

Karl's body tensed and he faced her. He swung his sword but she dodged. He blocked a thrust with his shield and deflected another swing, but she was too fast and her sword too powerful. Before he could think of his next move, she was in the middle of hers.

They fought over graves and around trees, leaving mementos to the deceased scattered behind them.

Ryza swung her sword down.

Karl pushed his shield against it, but he couldn't keep this up and pain shot through his arm. There was never an opening and she never got frustrated. His training was worthless and delayed the inevitable.

Arazod laughed.

Ryza shuffled a talon, so Karl swung his sword at her neck, but she knocked his blade away. She bashed his shield until he fell to his knees and dropped his protection.

Karl was so close to seeing his mother again, and took small comfort in the knowledge that they'd be reunited in the Realm of the Dead. He looked into Ryza's eyes. 'It's a shame Arazod didn't kill you along with your father.'

Ryza's eyes burned. She thrust her sword towards Karl's face, but he was knocked to the soil.

Karl lifted his head from the dirt.

Sags was skewered through the chest.

'Sags!' Karl's breath caught in his throat and everything was blurry.

Ryza pressed her talons against Sags' stomach and kicked him off her sword. The small blades of her weapon ripped Sags' chest open and bits of his flesh hung off them.

Sags dropped to his knees and fell face first onto the soil, his blood colouring it.

Ryza turned to Karl.

He wanted to chop her beak off. He searched for his sword but it was too far.

Ryza raised her blade. 'Now I'll do what my useless little brother couldn't.'

A glass bottle smashed against Ryza's armour and filled the area with smoke.

'Cowards!' Ryza called out.

'No!' Karl shouted. 'Where are you? I'll rip your head off!' He reached his arms out, trying to grab anything, and found his shield. His head was hot and terror filled his heart. 'Sags!' he called out.

An arm grabbed Karl and dragged him away.

A FRIEND FOR LIFE

*I*t was Karl's fault. All his fault.

Sags' limp body rested on a broken tree stump. His dark skin was dull and his breath was slow, too slow.

Frong removed Sags' blood-soaked undershirt. Sags' life flowed from the jagged wound by his heart, down the bark and dotted the soil.

Please don't die. You can't die.

Frong knelt on the soil and squeezed Sags' hand, pressing his forehead to his knuckles. 'Stay with us, Sags.'

Marlens rummaged through her sack of bottles. 'Come on, come on.' She pulled at her hair, mumbling different combinations of ingredients.

Sags grabbed the necklace around Frong's neck. 'It's okay. I'm not going anywhere until we're married.' He smiled through bloody teeth.

Karl swallowed the lump in his throat, wishing he'd choke on it.

Sags closed his eyes and groaned, so vulnerable.

'Come on, Marlens,' Frong said. He glanced at Karl, his eyes full of anger and hurt, but he didn't say anything. He turned back to his wounded lover.

Karl wished he could swap places with Sags.

Marlens placed three jars on the soil – one full of black thorns, the second a red powder, and the third a white sludge. 'Okay, hopefully this does it.'

Marlens took a small steel pot from her sack and poured the sludge into it. She grabbed a jar of orange liquid and poured it in a circle on the soil, starting a fire. She inhaled, placed the pot in the circle and sprinkled a pinch of red powder into it. Once it bubbled, Marlens counted twelve black thorns and dropped them into the mixture. She stirred it with a twig until it blended into a purple liquid, bubbled and glowed.

Frong removed his armour and undershirt. 'I think you'll need this.' He stuffed the shirt into Sags' mouth and held his hand. 'Crush my bones if you have to.'

Karl wanted to get closer but didn't dare.

Marlens took a cloth, grabbed the steaming pot and placed it next to Sags. She stroked his sweating forehead. 'I love you, old chum.'

Sags nodded.

Karl held his fist to his mouth.

Marlens lifted the pot and poured its contents into Sags' fleshy hole.

Sags bit down on Frong's undershirt. His body arched and his eyes bulged. The liquid fizzed and brown smoke billowed from the wound.

Karl wanted to turn away, but he had to watch, because it was his fault.

Frong stroked Sags' face. 'It's okay. It's okay.'

First Karl's mother, now one of his best friends, both stabbed to protect him. Why did people die for him? No, they died because of him.

Marlens tapped the pot. The last of the liquid dropped into

Sags. His eyes rolled into his head and his body relaxed. 'Help me turn him,' she said, her face stretched by pain.

She and Frong rolled Sags onto his side.

The stench of Sags' burning flesh hung in the air.

Frong rubbed Sags' neck. 'You did great.'

Sags spat the undershirt out and saliva ran down his cheek. He groaned; it was like a punch to Karl's heart.

Marlens took an orange leaf from a jar and rubbed it into Sags' gums until he passed out. She wiped her sweaty hair out of her eyes and removed her armour, fanning herself with her drenched undershirt. 'Okay, next bit.' She grabbed the loose flaps of skin on Sags' back and pinched them together to close the wound. 'Karl, pour that green and pink mixture of leech mouths over this line.' She pointed to the join of Sags' skin flaps.

Karl took the bottle in his shaking hands and poured the thick, lumpy liquid over the flaps. He watched the leech mouths bind the skin like metals being welded.

Marlens shook her head. 'I wish I had stronger potions, but this is the best I got in me.' She bit her lip.

'You're amazing.' Frong looked into her eyes.

Sabrinia emerged from the trees carrying water in Karl's helmet, but she didn't acknowledge him. She approached Marlens. 'How is he?' She handed Marlens the helmet.

Marlens rolled Sags onto his back and poured water into his wound. 'He's fighting.'

Frong pulled on his beard and wiped his eyes.

'I need more skin.' Marlens tried to seal Sags' chest wound, but the skin wouldn't meet and her finger poked into Sags' flesh.

Karl winced. 'Use mine.' He offered his arm.

'No.' Frong took a dagger from his boot. He closed his eyes and cut hairy skin from his thigh. He handed the bloody flap to Marlens.

She soaked it in the water in the helmet and placed it over

Sags' wound. She grabbed the potion bottle from Karl and poured it on, sealing the hole. 'Now we hope.'

Sags' chest rose and fell. So fragile.

Frong clasped his hands. 'Please.'

Sags' breathing slowed and then stopped.

Marlens pressed her ear to Sags' mouth and touched her fingers to his neck. She looked at the ground.

Why did she look at the ground?

'No...' Frong said.

Karl's heart clenched.

'Look.' Sabrinia pointed to Sags' hands opening and closing.

Karl's body lightened, dizzy from his emotions being hammered. 'He's okay. He's okay!'

Sags blinked and looked around. 'Thank you.' He smiled.

Marlens put a hand to her mouth and tears danced in her eyes.

Sabrinia put an arm around her.

'Sags!' Frong wept. 'You did it, Marlens.' He pressed his face to Sags' arm.

Sags stroked Frong's head and groaned. 'I've decided I want a cake made of mole-rat hair at our wedding.'

Frong chuckled. 'Anything you want. Even that terrible troupe of tree people you love who sing those morbid songs you love.'

Sags laughed. 'You all heard him say that. No backing out now.'

Karl burst into tears. 'I'm so sorry, Sags. I'm so sorry.'

Sags grabbed Karl's hand. 'Seems you need a bit more training yet.' He chuckled and coughed.

Karl smiled. 'Then you'd better recover soon so we can get back to it.'

Sags looked into his eyes. 'I'm glad you're okay.' He coughed again then choked. His eyes widened and his grip weakened.

'Sags?' Karl said.

Marlens nudged Karl out of the way and took Sags' hands. 'Sags? What's wrong?' She held the back of Sags' hand to her face and tapped it. 'He's goin' cold.'

Sags' lips whitened and his veins turned a dull grey. His body twitched.

Frong held Sags in a seated position. 'Sags. I've got you.' He rubbed and tapped Sags' chest to help him cough.

'Sags, no…' Karl trembled.

Frong kissed Sags' cheeks. 'Hold on, Sags. We'll find something.' Frong looked at Marlens. She stared at her bottles and shook her head.

Frong placed Sags' head on his lap and looked down at him.

Sags' eyes watered. 'I love you all.' He coughed blood. 'Thank you, Frong, for being you. Never stop expanding your world.' He put his hand on Frong's.

Frong squeezed him. 'We need to do it together. It's not an adventure without you.'

Sags nodded. 'Then don't forget me.' He ran a finger under Frong's eye. 'I love you, Frong. I'll miss your stories.'

'Please, Sags.' Frong gave him one last kiss.

The sparkle of life left Sags' eyes. His stomach deflated and his breathing stopped.

Frong stared at his fallen lover.

A numbness gripped Karl's body. It was like winter had started but only inside him.

'Sags…' Marlens stared at Sags.

Sabrinia held her.

There lay Karl's friend, once smiling and full of energy, now a shell. The crackling of Marlens' fire fought against the torturous silence.

Karl wanted to comfort Frong. 'Frong—'

Frong raised a hand, not even turning to Karl. 'Just… Just leave us, Karl. I don't want to say anything I regret.'

Karl nodded and walked into the forest.

SETTLING DUST

$\mathcal{A}$razod held Quizmal on a chain while Man-Hawks pecked at the flesh of dead Flowfornians.

Arazod turned to Ryza and took a breath. Maybe in the heat of battle she hadn't heard Karl. He couldn't risk it. 'I never killed Father. It was just a story that spread.' He wheezed.

She shook her head. 'Worry not, Little Arazod. I'm not going to listen to a human.' She shrugged. 'Plus, the story probably made you seem more powerful, and you need that.'

Arazod dug his talons into the pebbles. She always belittled him. He tugged at Quizmal's chains. 'What do I do with this thing?'

Quizmal bit him.

'Argh!' Arazod shook him off.

Ryza smirked. She nodded at a Man-Hawk, Karza, who approached. 'Lock it up until we no longer need it.'

Karza nodded and took the chain from Arazod.

'Wait.' Ryza crouched, her head level with Quizmal's. 'Biting Little Arazod was amusing. But you never attack a Man-Hawk.' She smiled like a parent would to a child, then swung a wing and slashed Quizmal's arm. He wept and blood ran from the gash. 'Get the runt out of my sight.'

'Yes, General Ryza.' Karza dragged Quizmal away.

Arnul flew towards Arazod and Ryza. He handed Ryza the Soul Bleeder.

Arazod's eyes lit up. 'My Soul Bleeder! Give it to me.'

Ryza held it out for Arazod.

He reached for his axe but she withdrew it and handed it back to Arnul. 'I think it's his now.'

Arnul smirked at Arazod. 'It's okay. You can have this sword instead.' He offered Arazod a shazaq.

Arazod reached for it, but Arnul threw it behind him to another Man-Hawk, Jaze.

'Sorry, Little Arazod. I was talking to Jaze,' Arnul said.

Arazod wished he was alone with Arnul. He would pluck and skin him.

Ryza patted Arazod's broken wing. 'It's best the ones who fly carry the big weapons.' She handed him a wooden club.

He'd gone from the only Man-Hawk to the reject among them once again. 'That makes sense,' Arazod said, because he had no choice.

Arnul took a pouch from inside his wing. 'I found something while gathering sticks.' He removed a green orb from the pouch and handed it to Ryza.

She held the orb to her eye. 'Well, hello there, Illuminus.'

'What's that?' Arazod asked.

Ryza smirked. 'The Soul of Illuminus. It's what Father and I were going to search for before I was attacked. This is the key to us being unstoppable.'

Arazod looked closely at the orb. He was sure he saw the woman inside it scream.

UNCONDITIONAL LOVE

A flapping cloud of feathery evil flew through the night towards the tiny parched island of Kanshar, northeast of Flowfornia.

Arazod had dreamed of commanding such glorious evil; instead he dreaded it.

Ryza held him under his arms as if he were a helpless baby Man-Hawk.

Arnul flew ahead and turned around. 'It's there.'

A dark, swirling wind blew around a cylindrical tower, covered in a layer of ice.

'Eratul's tower,' Ryza said.

Arnul, Ryza, Arazod and another nine Man-Hawks descended, stopping about thirty paces from the giant stone door.

The grass and soil were dry and hot, but a perfect circle of snow, three feet high, surrounded the tower.

Ryza walked towards the tower. 'We will awaken Death, and then command him to kill anyone who even looks at us the wrong way. With him, we make the rules. We build a world we want and the rest obey or die.' She stepped from the grass into the snow and dark wind. Her feathers blew chaotically and she held her chest and coughed. She leapt back onto the grass, her eyes bloodshot with panic.

Arazod had only seen that expression when Lord Ragnus twisted her neck.

Arnul rushed over to her and held her. 'What is it?'

She shook him off and caught her breath. 'Something isn't right.' She plucked a feather from her leg and dropped it. It fell like a stone and shattered. 'Frost magic.'

'Make a fire,' Arnul commanded the others. Three Man-Hawks nodded and opened a sack of supplies containing weapons, sticks, and food. They prepared a fire.

Arnul approached the snowy line and stretched his arm into the dark of the wind. His feathers blew and he retracted his arm, the tips of his feathers frozen.

Ryza flew up and tried to approach from the sky, but was faced with the same problem. 'Gah! It's like a hurricane of ice.'

A Man-Hawk handed Ryza a torch. She turned to Arazod. 'Little Arazod. Take this and see how far you get. Tell us what you see.'

Arazod took the torch and stared at it. 'What's this going to do?'

Arnul smirked at him and Ryza didn't seem to care.

He'd freeze to death, but maybe bravery was the path to acceptance. He stretched his free arm in front of him and a chill bit his claws. His nerves stung, stabbed by icy knives, and he coughed as if his throat wanted to leave his neck. This was a suicide mission. He stepped back, his beak trembling.

'What are you doing?' Ryza asked.

'It would be better to send someone who can fly. They can get in and out faster.' He wrapped his working wing around his body and rubbed it up and down his arm.

Ryza's beak twitched. 'Coward.' She snatched the torch from Arazod and handed it to a Man-Hawk, Felzun. 'But he's right.'

Felzun nodded. 'It would be my pleasure, General.'

That's all Arazod wanted; to be respected like that. Even when Ryza and his father were gone, he was entitled to become the Supreme Man-Hawk and they were meant to accept him by Man-Hawk law, but they mocked him because his broken wing made him different.

Felzun flew into the magic. The faint light of the torch extinguished and her silhouette froze and crashed to the floor. The scream and shattering drove Ryza to leap in and pull Felzun out.

Ryza collapsed, dotted with blood from where her skin cracked.

Arnul and the others surrounded Ryza and Felzun and warmed them with their wings.

Arazod stared at the red patches of snow where pieces of Felzun's leg were buried.

Ryza called two Man-Hawks over, Rezna and Hix. 'Take her back and get her fixed.'

They lifted Felzun's unconscious body and flew away, her wound already frozen shut.

'What do we do?' Arnul asked.

Ryza stood. 'We'll never get in there like this.'

'We need magic of our own,' he said.

She rubbed her feathers. 'The Gauntlet of Seliria.'

They flew back over Flowforn Forest, towards the castle.

Ryza carried Arazod and didn't say a word.

He wasn't sure whether that was good or a bad. At least she wasn't insulting him or calling him Little Arazod.

'There,' Ryza said. She and the remaining Man-Hawks descended into an open area by a stream.

'What's there?' Arazod asked.

Ryza dropped him from so high his ankle cracked against the hard mud.

'Argh!' Pain shot through his leg.

Ryza landed in front of him and smiled. 'Sorry, Little Arazod. Clumsy me.'

The Man-Hawks circled Arazod and screeched, creating a tornado of noise and terror.

Ryza's hand moved to the Grave Blade's grip.

'No.' Arazod crawled away. 'I didn't kill him. I told you.'

Ryza stepped towards him. 'I believe in using my enemies until they no longer serve a purpose.'

'Enemy?'

She shrugged. 'You can't fly. You don't follow orders. And worse yet, you tried to kill me.'

His heart raced and his feathers stood on end. 'No, no—'

Ryza dug her talons into Arazod's wounded ankle. He screamed into the night. She unsheathed the Grave Blade and dug it into the dirt between his legs. The blades welded into its side all faced him. 'One of the last things I saw when that freak twisted my neck was your little head poking out from behind some rocks. And it wasn't poking out to see if it was a good time to rescue me. Your little beak was smiling.'

She had known the whole time. Arazod searched the circle of Man-Hawks for a sympathetic face. They all smiled. 'Please. I was stupid in the past. I'm ready to serve you with all my loyalty. We can make the Man-Hawks great again.' He struggled to his knees and bowed his head.

She kicked him in the chest, leaving bloody dots where her talons pierced his skin. 'To be fair to you, I would have done the same if I had to clean our father's dung nest while you enjoyed gifts and everyone's respect.'

Arazod pushed himself to his feet and hobbled away, but Arnul shoved him back towards Ryza.

He fell in front of her. 'Please, Ryza. We're family.'

She smirked and held his chin. 'Apparently you don't have any siblings.' She raked her claws from the top of his head all the way down his face. The screeches of the Man-Hawks grew wilder, ringing in his ears. Blood covered his eyes.

Arazod turned to flee but pain ripped through his working wing. The Grave Blade poked through it. 'Wh… What?' His legs weakened.

The blade jerked upwards and tore his wing off.

He screamed and fell to his knees. His wing thudded onto the soil in front of him.

Claws gripped the top of Arazod's head. He knew what was coming and could do nothing about it.

'You've never been one of us,' Ryza said.

'Mercy,' he pleaded. 'Mercy.'

The sword pierced his broken wing and blood filled his mouth. Ryza's blade sawed back and forth until his wing came off.

Arazod fell beak first onto the soil. Pain was everywhere.

Ryza's talons dug into his back and she spat on the back of his head. The other Man-Hawks spat all over him.

He turned his aching neck to his side. The point of the Grave Blade dug into the mud by Ryza's talons.

She kneeled and smiled. 'I don't want to kill you, Little Arazod. That would be too kind.' Her eyes showed only hatred. 'I want you to die.' She stood and kicked him in the face.

His body burned warm and stung cold. He stared at his wings. Arnul picked them up and threw them into the stream. They floated away, leaving a bloody trail.

Arazod closed his eyes and felt every tingle of pain, compounded by the agony of rejection. He wished he had run into the icy hurricane.

TEAMWORK

Karl sat cross-legged against a tree stump and stared at the night sun. Tears rolled down his face. Just like that, life stopped. Earlier in the day Sags was getting married, probably planning everything and imagining a future. Now he was gone. How could life blow out as easily as a candle? Worse yet, everything else continued moving as though Sags didn't matter.

'Life is death,' Karl muttered Illuminus' words. 'Life is death.' That's all life was; a journey towards death, covered in deaths until it was time for your own death. He closed his eyes and rested his head.

Illuminus' screaming face crashed into Karl's mind. She screamed the words until they rang in his ears and made him sweat. Her face reddened and she pointed at him. His head throbbed.

'Karl…' A hand touched his shoulder. 'Karl,' Sabrinia said.

Illuminus disappeared and he opened his eyes.

'Are you okay?' Sabrinia asked.

He reached for her hand but she pulled it away. 'I'm as okay as I can be.'

She folded her arms and huffed. 'Why? Why didn't you run when I called out to you?'

He swallowed. 'Because I was trying to bring my mum back to life.'

'What?'

'That orb you saw me holding. It has the power to resurrect someone.' He hung his head, wanting to avoid her reaction. 'I lied to you, because if I told you what it did, and then saw even a hint in your eyes that you might want it to bring your dad back, I would've given it to you.' He swallowed and hoped for understanding.

She looked at the grass. 'Sags died because you were being selfish.'

Karl stood and stepped towards her but she raised her palm.

'If you had a chance to bring back someone you loved, you would've done the same,' Karl said.

She scratched her arm in that way she did when she was uncomfortable. Her disappointed eyes locked on his. 'That's the difference, Karl. In that situation, with life on the line, I would have let her go.'

Karl shook his head. 'You don't know that. Unless you're the one in the situation, you don't know.'

'I do, because I put others before myself.'

He needed to let her vent so he took a breath, but the tension built inside him. 'Yes, it's all about duty to others. So much so that you never do anything for yourself.'

'What do you mean by that?' She stared at him.

He'd made it clear enough he was talking about her marriage to Arazod. Karl turned his back on her and focused on the night sun, unsure of what to say. He'd said enough.

'Well, I'd rather live setting an example to others than be the reason they die.'

Karl's body deflated. She was right. He closed his eyes until her steps faded away. He sat on the grass, lay back and rested his head against it. He decided to sleep and hoped that when he woke up it would all be different. He closed his eyes and drifted.

Life is death.

Karl stood alone on green sand on the shore. Green fog rose around him and green fibres throbbed on the horizon like a barrier between him and the world. He turned and Illuminus leapt on him, knocking him down. 'Life is death.' She punched his chest and scratched his face. 'Life is death, life is death.'

He tried to shout, but no words formed. His heartbeat echoed around him until it was so loud his head stung.

Illuminus lifted her hand for one final strike.

Karl woke up confused, sweating, his breath fast and his chest heavy. He wiped his forehead. *Life is death.* It must be her protesting, knowing that because she's a rune, as soon as she's used, she'll die. He had to use her though. He was so close to being with his mother again, but he had to accept that wouldn't happen, because he needed to bring Sags back to life.

Karl crept by Sabrinia while she stared at the castle, no doubt thinking about her people. He picked up his helmet, put it on and strapped his shield to his back.

Marlens slept at the foot of the stump where Sags lay. Her eyes twitched as though in a nightmare.

Poor Frong kneeled by Sags, held his hand and rubbed his forehead. 'I'll go back to Vasen and spend my sunsets at the table where we met. You remember? The sun stroked the yellow beads that hung from the tavern posts. I was eating fresh berries and you snatched one from me and ate it. I thought you were going to attack me, but it was simply your strange way of saying hello because you were nervous. Then I told you to go away and you did, but luckily we met again.'

Karl bit his bottom lip. He strode through the forest towards Flowforn. He would make things right.

Man-Hawks patrolled the skies. He couldn't figure out a safe way in, but maybe if he snuck over the boulder by the collapsed wall he could take shelter in the tavern and work out the next stage of the plan. If he was lucky, the Soul of Illuminus was still in the cemetery.

He waited until a Man-Hawk flew away. He stepped out of the cover of trees but a strong arm wrapped around his neck and pulled him back.

'What do you think you're doing?' Frong said.

'I'm getting him back.' Karl struggled against Frong's grip.

Frong turned Karl and pushed him against a tree to face him. 'You don't even have a weapon!' Frong clenched his fist and his eyes burned into Karl. 'He died to save you and you want to throw away that gift?'

Karl's face was hot and tears filled his eyes. 'I don't care if I die. I'll get the soul and throw it over the wall to you and you take it to him. It doesn't matter what happens to me. I just want him back. If I wasn't selfish, if I wasn't so desperate, then—'

Frong pulled Karl into a hug.

Karl wept into Frong's shoulder. 'I'm sorry—'

'Shh.' Frong squeezed him. 'Just…' Frong should have been punching him, but as always, he was full of love.

'What's going on?' Sabrinia asked.

Frong released Karl but kept an arm on his shoulder. 'He wants to recover the soul to save Sags. I won't let him.'

Sabrinia nodded. 'Running in there would be stupid. One stupid decision has already cost us.'

Her words stung.

She gazed at her broken home. 'But we do need to resurrect Sags. And we do need to save innocent people before there are any more casualties.'

Frong nodded. 'What do you propose we do?'

Sabrinia pulled at her hair and narrowed her eyes. 'As much as I want to rush in there, trying to fight them would be suicide. The other option we have won't be much better.' She gazed away from Flowforn. 'Southeast is Barma, the home of the Barmashin tribe. They wanted to live in Flowforn, but my father turned them away because of their bizarre customs and beliefs.'

'What if they find the soul?' Karl said, not wanting to leave when they were so close.

'We need to hope that if they do, they don't know what to do with it,' she answered.

'We can't risk it. What if we find the others?' Karl said. 'Bar Witch, Hargon; where are they?'

Sabrinia shook her head. 'We could end up looking for days and we need more than them to turn this in our favour. As much as I hate it, an alliance is our best hope.'

Karl turned to Frong who seemed equally unsure. King Sastin had cut off all alliances and Karl doubted anyone would risk their people for the sake of a kingdom that had turned its back on them.

He hoped Sabrinia knew what she was doing.

AN UNWANTED REUNION

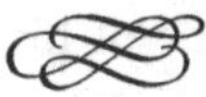

Oaf and Questions followed the stream through the sunny forest.

Oaf gazed at the side of Questions' head. 'Do you blame me?'

She'd barely asked him anything for two sunsets. She stared at the ground and creased her forehead, but then shook her head.

'I blame me.' He wished she'd shout at him or hit him. Or do something other than suffer in silence. He wished she'd ask him a weird question about the clouds or why soil was brown. Anything. Oaf opened his water pouch and drank. He offered Questions some but she ignored it.

She took the blade the Fool had given her and waved some flies away. 'Where is he?'

'I don't know. But Karl and the others will help.'

Questions nodded and turned to him. 'Will you be able to kill?'

That was the question he dreaded. It was in his blood to preserve life, not to murder, but in this situation things were different. 'For our son, I'll rip the heads off a thousand Man-Hawks.' He hoped if it came to it he wouldn't hesitate.

Questions nodded. She stopped and pointed to a bloody

streak that ran from the muddy grass to a rock by the stream. She put her hand to her mouth. 'Do you think?'

Oaf's neck tensed. 'No. He's alive. We're going to find him.' He didn't want to look but they followed the blood. Oaf walked around the rock. The image his mind created caused vomit to rise in his mouth. His terror turned to anger. 'You!'

Arazod laid there, the side of his face in the stream and his back feathers soaked in blood. Water flowed around his face and beak and he groaned.

Questions joined Oaf, her face turned red. 'Do you think he knows something?'

Oaf lifted Arazod and tossed him against a broken tree stump. 'Talk.'

Arazod covered his head and struggled to breathe.

Oaf grabbed Arazod's neck. 'What has your sister done with our son?'

Arazod wheezed and groaned. His left eye twitched.

'Shall we clean him so he's well enough to speak?' Questions asked.

Oaf nodded and removed his cloak. He ripped Arazod's armour off, carried him into the stream and dipped him in the water. Arazod's eyes fluttered and his beak twisted when stream water met his wounds.

Questions ripped her sleeve, dunked it in the water and wiped Arazod's lacerations clean. She took some berries from her pocket and put them into Arazod's beak. He weakly chewed and swallowed them.

'Can you lift him higher?' Questions asked.

Oaf did, and Questions cleaned Arazod's back.

They returned to the rock and laid Arazod against it. Oaf ripped strips from his cloak and wrapped Arazod's injuries.

Questions made a fire and they waited for Arazod to awaken, if he would. They held hands and stared at him. The night sun rose before he showed any sign of life.

Arazod looked at Oaf with misery in his eyes. He raised a claw. 'Kill… me…'

Oaf leaned over him. 'Where is our son?'

Arazod shook his head.

Oaf squeezed Arazod's face and yelled into it. 'Where is our son?'

Arazod whined.

Questions placed a hand on Oaf's arm. He took a breath and released Arazod's face.

Arazod wheezed. 'Flowforn…'

Oaf nodded and stood. 'Let's go, Questions.' He had no issue with leaving Arazod. They walked away.

'Wait,' Arazod called out weakly. 'Listen.'

Oaf stopped. 'What?'

'War. Flowforn isn't safe.' He wheezed.

Questions stepped towards Arazod. 'How do we get our son?'

'Sister won't kill him… until she's powerful.' He coughed blood on himself. 'In case she… needs him.' He fell to the side. 'Your friends… escaped. No idea where.'

Oaf turned to Questions. 'What do we do?'

'Shall we look for them?'

'How do we even find them?' He clenched his fists. 'We have to go to the castle and find our boy. Maybe we'll find survivors on the way.'

Arazod raised an arm. 'Please, kill me. Please.'

Oaf turned to Questions, who gripped her dagger.

Killing wasn't in her, but her normally gentle face twisted with anger and pain.

BABYSITTING

Noise filled the stuffy, secret room in the tavern. Tears, fear and uncertainty mixed into a buzz that whirred around Bar Witch's head. She stood by a plinth with a tinderbox on it.

The point of the secret room was to only open from one side. In trying to save everyone, she had locked them in a big brick coffin. 'Quiet, everyone. Try to stay calm.' The noise lowered but was still too loud for her liking.

'When are we getting out?' a bald man asked her.

'I'm hungry, where's the food? And water, we need water,' a small, filthy-looking boy whined.

'Are we going to die?' an annoying girl who always complained about Bar Witch's ale asked.

In every direction was unpleasant noise. She could handle cranky people and tears from behind the bar, because she could drown them in a drink, but here, she was lost. She raised an arm. 'I don't have the answer to any of your questions, so best to just be quiet for a bit.'

'But you made us come in here,' a drunk idiot said.

'Would you rather be out there?'

The idiot looked at the stone floor.

'Listen,' Bar Witch said. 'We all need to keep calm. If you need patching up, see that red-haired one.' She pointed at Hargon, who used the hair of the wizard-lizard to regenerate a girl's hand. 'Help should be coming soon.' Bar Witch had no idea if that was true.

The people left her alone. She closed her eyes, but a baby cried. Bar Witch looked around for the noise and found the baby lying in the corner. 'Sort that out, someone!'

Everyone looked at each other. A short man, holding a bloody rag to his neck, came forward. His face was pale and sweat streaked his cheeks. 'I found him lying in some hay. His parents must've ditched him to run.' He could hardly breathe.

Bar Witch folded her arms. 'Well then, he's yours.'

'I'm not sure that's how it works,' he said.

'You found him and brought him here. Sounds about right to me.' She patted his shoulder but he collapsed, dead. Flowfornians gasped and backed away.

'That's not from me touching him,' she clarified. How were they going to survive? There were too many problems. For all she knew, everything outside was on fire and everyone had been killed. She wished she had a barrel of ale.

Proster, a dark-haired brute and builder, stepped forward. 'Someone help me move him. We'll bury him when we're free.'

A woman helped him to carry the dead man away.

Bar Witch approached the baby, picked him up and then turned to everyone. 'The most important thing we can do is stay quiet.' She wasn't sure what she was supposed to do with the life in her hands. 'There, there, quiet now.'

The baby's cries grew louder. That's why she couldn't stand them. At least people would say what they wanted, even if it was slurred or annoying. Babies had some stupid crying code instead. Bar Witch thought about performing some of her party magic, but the space was too small and might lead to chaos.

Hargon came over. 'Need a hand?'

Bar Witch handed him the baby. 'Please take it. I'm an entertainer to drunks, not a leader to morons or a baby minder.'

Hargon swapped the baby for the hair of the wizard-lizard. He rocked the baby and made bizarre noises. 'Why don't you just treat this lot like a drunk audience?' Hargon asked Bar Witch.

She scowled. 'A group this size will go wrong. For every person that likes something, another four will hate it.'

The baby fell asleep and Hargon smiled. 'I always wanted to be a dad.' He stroked the baby's head. 'Closest I got was a chicken.'

Maybe Bar Witch should be nicer to him. He was an idiot, but an innocent one. 'Yeah? What was it called?'

Hargon nodded. 'Chicky. My dad wasn't the most creative with names. And just when I was learning what Chicky's different noises meant, we had to eat him.' Hargon shrugged. 'But I like to think he tasted so good because he died happy.'

Bar Witch shook her head. Her eyes widened and she pressed her ear to the bricks, raising her arm for everyone to be quiet.

Muffled conversation seeped through the bricks.

'Is it help?' the annoying girl asked.

Bar Witch turned to her and pressed her finger to her lips. She turned back to the wall and listened.

'There's nobody in the tavern,' a whiny voice said.

'But I saw them. Loads of them, and so did Arnul. They couldn't have just vanished,' the other replied and squawked.

'Stop wasting my time. I want to go and peck more humans.'

Bar Witch exhaled, relieved. She turned back to the people but knocked into the tinderbox. It crashed against the floor. She stood stone still but the baby cried.

Peezant perched on a branch and looked down at the tavern. Two Man-Hawks pointed to the outer wall.

'See! It came from the wall,' the taller Man-Hawk said.

'But the place is empty and walls don't cry,' the whiny one replied.

'How do you know? Have you met all the walls in the world?' The taller one poked its sword between the bricks.

'Well, no, but—'

'We were locked up for years. Maybe a new type of brick has been magicked and this one has some kind of secret.'

The Man-Hawk grunted. 'Let's smash it. At least then if it is a talking wall it'll shut up.'

Peezant turned and looked into the forest. 'Peezant,' he squawked and flew away from the castle, hoping to find help before it was too late.

SAND, SEA AND SCREAMS

Karl and the others waded through a muddy bog that, thanks to the scorching sun, was more like a hot stew.

Karl and Frong carried Sags on tied-together planks they had taken from an abandoned cart. Frong wanted to carry Sags from the feet so he could look at his face. They were so desperate to preserve him that they panicked whenever insects hovered around Sags' corpse.

Frong kept speaking to Sags. It was as if he was convinced Sags would spring back into life and reply at any moment.

It made Karl think about why people buried the dead. Maybe it was knowing they were close. Even though they were dead it kept hope alive. It was how he felt about his mum. To him, she was perfectly preserved underground and perhaps, even without a relic, she might just rise from the soil one day.

Sabrinia walked ahead, out of the bog and onto the endless sand. She'd barely spoken to Karl the entire journey. The only conversations they had were functional, about rest and food.

Their destination appeared, a speck on the sandy horizon, still too far away.

Karl turned to Frong. 'You okay?'

Frong nodded. 'Thanks.'

'Marlens?' Karl asked.

She nodded with a half smile and continued walking with her head down.

Karl and Frong climbed out of the bog. They set Sags down, poured some water on him and sat for a moment.

Behind Karl, the tallest yellow stone walls he'd come across reached into the sky. A shriek came from beyond them, shaking him to his core. 'What was that?'

Frong scratched his beard. 'That's the reason we came by the messy route.' He took a breath. 'Jermal. The most advanced people in Hastovia, but unfortunately ones who made bad decisions.' He stood and lifted his side of Sags' planks.

They resumed their journey and Frong continued his story. 'Their leader made a deal with the Spirit Queen, a being corrupted by Shardur, the god of shadow and darkness, and that was the end of their people.'

'And that shriek?' Karl asked.

'The result of the deal.' For once, Frong didn't seem interested in continuing a story and Karl wasn't sure he wanted to know any more.

'Stop.' Sabrinia held her hand over her eyes.

From their destination, figures rode towards them on strange-looking horses that had humps growing out of their sides.

'Humped horses,' Frong said.

Sabrinia stood in front of everyone to greet the six riders.

They were huge clumps of muscle in light sheets. They pointed their curved swords at Karl and the group.

Sabrinia raised her hands and placed her bow on the sand, followed by her quiver of arrows. 'Let's start with peace and hopefully we'll end up with friends,' she told her allies.

The others followed her lead. Karl and Frong placed Sags

down. Karl removed his shield and tossed it on the sand, while Frong removed his spear and Sags' throwing axes. Marlens removed her potion belt and dropped her sack.

The warriors spoke in a language of aggressive noises. Karl hoped the meaning didn't match the sound.

Sabrinia stepped towards one of them. 'I've no idea what you're saying, but we would like to see your king.' She moved her hands up and down above her head to suggest a crown.

The warriors looked at each other. One sprang off his humped horse, flipping and landing on his feet as though such a manoeuvre was nothing. He held his sword and approached the weapons, picking them up and throwing them to his warrior friends.

'Gulrit.' He nodded at Sabrinia.

'Gulrit?' she replied.

He stretched his arms out and clenched his fists, so Sabrinia copied him.

The warrior reached into a sack on the humped horse and retrieved a rope.

Karl stepped forwards. 'No—'

'It's okay,' Sabrinia said. 'It's probably just a precaution. I suggest we all do this… gulrit.'

The warrior tied her wrists, and the other warriors tied the rest of the group. Two warriors took Sags.

'Please be careful with him.' Frong welled up.

'He'll be fine,' Karl said.

They placed Sags on the back of a humped horse and each took a prisoner and rode in the direction they came from.

Karl looked up at the sky and was sure he saw Peezant.

The warrior pulled a sack over Karl's head and tied it.

Karl struggled to breathe and worried they had made a terrible mistake.

A FRENEMY IN NEED

Sabrinia shuffled her knees on the creaky, wooden floor of a stuffy room. With every inhalation the sandy sack invaded her mouth and any footsteps made her think a sword was about to slice her head off.

Someone yanked the sack off her head and she took a breath. She faced a luxurious throne covered in cushions. It was the only luxurious thing in the hall. The green decay of wood sickness ate the walls.

The warriors stood behind her and her friends. If the warriors were going to kill them it would've happened by now. It didn't make the cold blade against the back of her neck any less terrifying.

Sabrinia noticed Karl scan the room, probably expecting the worst. His face filled her with rage, but maybe he was right and she would have done the same if she had the orb. Everyone could imagine what they would do with power, but they couldn't truly know until they had it. It didn't change that Karl had done something stupid and costly.

A wooden door creaked open and a large half-naked man with long brown hair under a wooden crown entered. A light sheet didn't do much to cover what was underneath and a steel rod ran from his left knee to the ground where a leg should be. He carried a steel axe over his shoulder, put it down by the throne and sat scratching his muscular stomach. He stared at Sabrinia and raised his steel leg onto a throne arm, drawing attention to what she didn't want to see.

'You can rise,' he said in a slow and precise tone. 'Jut kul pulfi,' he said to his warriors.

A warrior grabbed Sabrinia by her bound wrists and pulled her to her feet.

'So why would anyone come all the way out here?' The man looked Sabrinia up and down.

Sabrinia held his gaze. 'I'm Princess Sabrinia of Flowforn, daughter of King Sastin, and I come wanting to put right the wrongs of the past. To apologise for how my father treated your people.'

He shrugged. 'Your Sastin didn't do anything to me. I'm Lord Lofad. Your father wronged my father, but who cares for the arguments of old idiots who are both gone.'

Sabrinia swallowed. 'I'm sorry. Losing a father is horrible.'

Lord Lofad shook his head. 'Mine didn't die; he fled. With most of our supplies, a handful of warriors and ships.'

Lofad was so relaxed about it. 'Then I'm sorry your kingdom has suffered its own tragedy,' Sabrinia said.

He lowered his leg to the floor and leaned forward. 'Please. Cut the politeness. I doubt you came all the way to this sandy dump to make friends without the need for something, so go on. And make it worth listening to.'

The warrior behind Karl tightened her grip around her curved sword. 'Well, I'm here to ask for your help.' Sabrinia told her story, mentioning everything from Arazod, Lord Ragnus and the Fools, to the latest invasion. Every detail was crucial to conveying the danger the Man-Hawks posed.

Lofad spun his axe handle as though it was more interesting.

He raised a hand to stop her speaking. 'Why should we care? They're never going to come out here.'

Sabrinia shrugged. 'You don't know that. You may have great warriors, but nothing will protect you when it rains boulders. Your wooden buildings will be reduced to splinters. So, you can wait and hope they leave your home alone, or you can come with us, to a place we know better than anyone else, and strike first.'

He smirked and ran his tongue over his teeth. 'I see your point, but this all comes down to one key detail.' He sat back. 'What's in it for me?'

'Survival,' Sabrinia said. 'We don't fight darkness to gain anything. It's to protect the future.'

Lofad laughed. Arrogance oozed out of him and Sabrinia wished she didn't have to put her hope in him.

'That sounds lovely,' Lofad said. 'But I like thinking about me and now. So I'll ask once more before we send you back into the desert. What is in it for me?'

Sabrinia took a step forward, followed by a warrior, but Lofad waved the warrior away. 'A new home,' Sabrinia said. 'It's clear this place isn't doing so well.' She gestured to the rotting walls. 'The luxuries a man of your position deserves seem to not extend beyond that chair and crown, and the sack over my head didn't stop me smelling the rotten fish on the way in or feeling the silent sadness over your kingdom. From my father's stories this was a place busy with trade, and you could hear the buzz of the markets from deep within the desert.' She shrugged. 'So, you can stay here and continue to watch your home crumble while no trade comes in and your warriors lose heart, or I can offer you a home, your own part of the castle, stables for your horses and happiness for your people.'

He stared at her and she stared at his axe, hoping he wouldn't swing it at her.

Lofad sighed, the bravado momentarily leaving him. 'We are sick of the sea winds. The snakes are irritating and the desert climate offers nothing but a dry throat and itchy skin.' He fanned his sheet. 'We want to be able to live without clothes, without worrying that sand will enter every part of us.'

Sabrinia grimaced at the image. Perhaps she'd build Lofad and his people a separate castle to spare Flowfornian eyes. 'So we have a deal?'

Lofad stared at her and nodded. 'Yes we do.'

Sabrinia smiled. Finally, something positive.

Lofad smirked. 'If you also agree to make me the ruler of Flowforn and you become my servant.'

'What?' She would've punched him in the eye if it wouldn't lead to her death. She swallowed her rage but couldn't think of a way out.

'You see, for me, rotting here comfortably is still a better option than you have, which is wandering like a stray from kingdom to kingdom, begging for help until you're either killed or taken as a prisoner.'

'Don't do it, Sabrinia,' Frong said.

Karl clenched his fists. She hoped he wouldn't do anything rash.

Marlens turned to Sabrinia. 'It's not worth it.'

To Sabrinia it was worth it if it meant saving her people.

She was about to agree but Karl interrupted. 'How about we give you something to help you get your leg back?' he said.

Sabrinia wished he'd kept his mouth shut.

In a flash, Lofad's axe was a hair away from Karl's throat. 'If you're mocking me, you won't have much time to regret it.'

'He's right,' Frong said. 'There's a magic item in the castle; the hair of the wizard-lizard.' Frong explained what it did and convinced Lofad to look at Sags' tongue.

Lofad ordered a warrior to open Sags' mouth and show him.

Lofad withdrew his weapon. 'I'm not enamoured by the colour, but okay. We have a deal if we get to live in Flowforn as you suggested, and you give me that magic item.'

Sabrinia was relieved but terrified. She didn't trust him but had to. What if the relic had been destroyed in the battle or Ryza had it? She wished Karl hadn't said anything.

Lofad added, 'But if you're lying about this item, I won't kill you.' He grinned. 'Instead, I'll hack the legs off all of you and drag your bodies around the desert while the hot sand chews at your flesh.' He approached Sabrinia and stared down at her. He pointed to Sags. 'Do you want us to bury your dead at sea as a show of solidarity?'

'We want to bury him back in Flowforn, his home,' Frong said.

Lofad nodded. He kissed Sabrinia's bound hands and nodded at his warriors. 'Shvit.'

They cut everyone's ropes, freeing the group.

'Why don't you untie the ropes? Cutting seems like a waste,' Karl said.

Lofad ignored Karl and walked to his wooden door. 'The sand gets vicious in the evenings, so tonight we rest. Tomorrow I'll gather seventy of my finest fighters and we will reclaim *our* Flowforn.'

TONGUE TIED

*K*arl stared out of the tiny hole in his wooden room, which felt more like a cell. The sun set over the sandy horizon beyond Barma. He couldn't wait for tomorrow to come so they could leave.

This place was so different from Flowforn. Back home, food was plentiful and people buzzed around the alleys. Here, there was barely a footprint in the sand and all Karl had to eat was a bowl of seeds.

He dropped some seeds into his mouth and sighed. Lofad had requested that they remain in their rooms, but Karl's thoughts were torturous. His mind cycled through images of his mum dying in his arms, Sags with a sword stuck in his chest, and Sabrinia's disappointed face.

He poked his head out of the door. A warrior disappeared around a corner, so Karl snuck outside.

Karl walked between the wooden huts towards the shore. Heat clogged the air and waves broke the eerie silence.

Maybe the waves would ease Karl's mind. He sat and remembered talking with his mother on the coast of Reech. It was brief but perfect. Her death flashed in his mind. The axe wound across her chest. The blood. The light in her eyes disappearing.

His chest ached and he walked away from the shore.

He passed a hut and something smashed into his side, knocking him through the hut door and the bowl of seeds out of his grip.

A hand covered his mouth and he fell to the floor. Whoever it was stayed on top of him, pressing Karl's stomach against the sand-covered wood. Karl expected an attack, but nothing came. He stopped struggling and held his arms out, trying to avoid inhaling the stench of his attacker's unwashed fingers.

Feet with fungus-covered nails stepped in front of Karl's face, then the knees came down and so did hands, ragged clothing and a frail old woman. She pressed her finger to her cracked lips.

Karl nodded, and whoever was on his back released their hand from his mouth.

Karl turned and a large bald boy pulled a wooden chair for him. Karl sat while the boy collected the seeds and handed Karl the bowl.

The boy and woman stared at Karl.

'I think you're meant to start the conversation,' Karl said. The room was bare.

The frail woman faced Karl and opened her mouth. Karl fought the urge to scream. She had no tongue.

The woman gestured for Karl to wait and she looked at the boy, who tapped the chair Karl sat on.

'It's all yours.' Karl stood.

The boy placed the chair sideways and stomped a leg off it. He took a splint and handed it to the frail woman.

Karl worried she was going to stab him so stepped back towards the door, but stopped when she cut her forearm. 'Are you sure that's a good idea?'

The boy grimaced. The woman wiped her finger in the blood and wrote on the wooden wall.

Karl worried she'd pass out from the amount of blood she had used. When she was done Karl read the word, 'Usurper.' Karl's heart thumped. 'Did Lord Lofad kill his father?'

The woman nodded, then crossed her wrists as though bound and pointed to her and the boy.

'You're prisoners?' Karl asked.

She nodded.

'And...' he pointed to his tongue.

The woman gestured it being sliced off.

Karl's body tensed. 'I'll tell my friends, and we'll help you.'

The boy tore fabric from his cloak and wrapped the woman's wound.

She cried at Karl's words and squeezed his hand, touching it to her forehead.

Their lives must have been miserable. 'I'll be back.' Karl opened the door to the hut. The hilt of a curved sword whacked the side of his head and the world stopped.

SECRET'S OUT

Bar Witch couldn't figure out how to wipe the look of panic off the faces of the eighty or so Flowfornians in her care, but she knew they couldn't hang around waiting for death to come to them.

'Psst,' Hargon called from the entrance to the secret room.

Bar Witch rushed over. 'Why are you psssting me?'

He stared at the entrance. 'It's them,' he whispered. He handed the sleeping baby to a young woman, who looked terrified. 'Best to stand over there.' He pointed her to the opposite end of the room.

Bar Witch edged closer to the door. Something smashed against the other side of it, likely a barrel.

'How can this place be empty!' a Man-Hawk with a gruff voice said. 'Nobody in the bar. Nobody in the cellar. Nobody in here!'

'Maybe we really are going mad,' the whiny voice said.

'But we heard it!' the gruff voice replied.

Bar Witch closed her eyes, relieved they might give up.

'Hold on,' the whiny one said. 'This stone. It moves under my weight. Look!'

Bar Witch swallowed a pin-like pain. Maybe she could convince everyone to swarm the Man-Hawks. There would be some Flowfornian casualties, but they'd overwhelm the Man-Hawks.

'This moves too!' the gruff one said.

Each secret stone they uncovered convinced Bar Witch her time on Hastovia was over. She thought of her regrets, like how she'd never travelled to the village she was sold from as a child. She wanted to learn more about her people.

'Why's nothing happening?' The Man-Hawks couldn't find the stone they needed to press, and their frustrated squawks said as much.

Bar Witch let herself hope. Maybe they'd give up.

'Right. Enough,' the gruff one said. 'Let's get a boulder and crush the whole place.'

Flowfornians shuffled into the corners.

The whiny voice spoke up. 'No! Let's get a battering ram. I want to personally stick my sword through whoever or whatever is messing with us.'

The gruff one laughed. 'Great idea.'

They left. What was less horrific, being stabbed, or being crushed? Bar Witch needed to reassure everyone so turned to them, careful to choose her words. 'Okay, I don't think—'

'We're finished!' the annoying girl said, annoyingly correct. 'It's your fault!'

The majority of the Flowfornians agreed with her.

'You dragged us in here,' the girl said.

Hargon and Proster stood by Bar Witch. Hargon raised his hands. 'We were trying to save you all.'

Proster turned his hammer in his hand. 'If we fight the Man-Hawks we can swarm them.'

The girl grabbed Bar Witch around the collar of her tunic. 'And she'll be right at the front.'

Bar Witch stared her down. She could drive her head into the girl's face from here, but she didn't want to cause a riot in such a confined space. She needed to be an example and to stop the revolt before it started, so she spoke calmly. 'If you don't let go of me now, I'll bite your nose off.'

The girl loosened her grip.

Bar Witch straightened her tunic. 'Of course I'll be at the front protecting you idiots, like I've been doing since those feathery morons brought the rocky rain.'

The door clicked and everyone froze. Had they found the way in? Bar Witch's eyes widened and she turned around. 'Stand back. This'll distract them so we can rush them!' She rolled her shoulders and her eyes shot into the back of her head. The pain warmed her. The blue glow flowed through her veins, down her arms, and into her wrists. 'Donkabal!' Bar Witch's eyes bulged and cracked. A yellow liquid sprayed out of them and stretched her eye sockets. Bar Witch fell into Hargon's arms.

The liquid moved and collected, forming a yellow ball the size of a barrel.

The door swung open, but nobody was there.

The ball opened its one big eye, rolled out of the door and into the back room. It crashed into the walls and anything it touched stuck to it. It squeaked and continued into the bar.

Hargon helped Bar Witch to stand and Proster went to investigate. He turned back and shrugged. 'Nothing.'

Peezant flew in and landed on Bar Witch's shoulder. 'Peezant!'

Bar Witch smiled through the pain, her breath slow.

Hargon beamed.

'We're free!' The annoying girl charged towards the door but Bar Witch held a weak arm out. 'Not yet.'

Peezant told them about what had happened to Karl and the others, and he warned them that Man-Hawks patrolled the sky above Flowforn.

'We'll find a way to sneak this lot out, then we'll join you,' Bar

Witch said. 'I'm sick to death of them anyway.' She looked at the girl.

'I have a plan,' Proster said.

Bar Witch and Hargon waited behind a barrel outside the secret room. Bar Witch gripped a splintered piece of barrel, ready to wedge it into a Man-Hawk.

'Do you think this'll work?' Hargon turned his makeshift dagger in his hand.

'Better than nothing.' She noticed Hargon's hands shaking.

He shuffled, his head moving between the door to the bar area and the door to the cellar. 'So how come you can do magic?'

Bar Witch huffed. Talking might calm him. 'I come from a weird group of people who live by a blessed or a cursed lake, depending which way you look at it. When we're newborns, some old idiot takes us to the lake and chucks us in it.'

'That's a bit harsh,' Hargon said.

'Yep. When we drown, our bodies either become one with this way of magic, or we die. Bit rubbish, really, not to be given a choice.'

'Yeah.' His eyes narrowed.

'And that's why my spells are so exhausting. Anything other than the basic ones, like vanishing cups or fancy lights for entertaining, use up life energy. We're meant to learn our spells from a book, but another old idiot took it and ran off, so the spells I know are all I'll ever have. I could say random words and see what happens, but that's pretty dangerous. Might stumble across a big one and croak.'

Hargon grimaced.

Proster entered from the bar area. 'They're coming.' He returned to put the plan into action.

Bar Witch listened out.

'Who are you?' Bar Witch heard the whiny Man-Hawk ask.

'I'm the owner,' Proster said. 'So unless you plan on buying a drink, I've got an idea for where you can shove that ram.'

'What did you say?' the gruff Man-Hawk responded.

Bar Witch looked at Hargon and nodded. They were ready.

'You heard me,' Proster said. Glass smashed and he ran through the back room and into the cellar, followed by two Man-Hawks.

'Let's make this count,' Bar Witch said, still weak from casting the spell.

They approached the cellar steps but the tavern door opened. A Man-Hawk faced them, sword drawn. She spread her wings and stretched her neck up.

Hargon lunged at her and stabbed her in the shoulder.

She dropped her sword, but clawed at his back and threw him down. She turned to pick up her sword, but Bar Witch had it and cut the Man-Hawk's head off. Bar Witch fell to her knees, exhausted and covered in spots of blood.

Hargon stared at Bar Witch, his breathing frantic. 'Thanks. Are you okay?'

She nodded and handed him the sword. 'We need to—' She pointed towards the cellar where growls of battle echoed.

They descended the steps.

Proster, backed into the corner, fended off both Man-Hawks.

Hargon ran towards him.

Bar Witch's weary legs struggled. They would never get to Proster in time.

The smaller Man-Hawk swung his sword at Proster's neck, but Proster deflected it with his hammer. He kicked the Man-Hawk in the chest, grabbed his feathered foe's wrist, snapped it back and took the sword. Proster sliced him across the face, turned and blocked a strike from the larger enemy, then swung back around and bashed the smaller Man-Hawk's head with the hammer.

'Proster, turn around!' Hargon yelled.

The larger Man-Hawk stabbed Proster through the back.

Bar Witch fell to her knees. 'No!'

Proster stared at the blade poking out of his stomach. His life poured out of his body. 'Get him, idiots.'

Hargon yelled and stabbed the Man-Hawk in the neck. He turned and held Proster, removed the sword and eased him to the floor. 'I've got you, I've got you.'

Bar Witch wished she had the strength to have gotten to Proster quicker. She crawled over and stared at Proster's face.

'We'll make it worth it, Proster.'

He was gone.

They sat for a moment. Although they had won this small battle, they felt only loss.

Hargon left, then returned with some Flowfornians to help them carry the bodies.

They piled the Man-Hawks into a corner of the secret room and lay Proster to rest by a wall.

Hargon tried to revive him using the hair of the wizard-lizard, and while the relic sealed the wound, it couldn't bring him back.

Peezant landed on Bar Witch's shoulder. 'The others need your help.'

She looked around the room at the hopelessness. She wanted to help her friends, but she couldn't sacrifice all these idiots. 'We need to look after this lot.'

Hargon lifted the baby and rocked him. 'They need us, Peezant.'

Peezant nodded understanding and pecked Bar Witch. 'Peezant.'

'Good luck. We'll join you as soon as we can,' Bar Witch said.

'Peezant,' Peezant said and flew away.

Bar Witch wanted to sleep, but they needed to escape, or to bring food and water to the others. She turned to the worried

Flowfornians. 'We're going to get food and water and find an escape route. We're going to have to lock you in, though. Any objections?' She fixed her eyes on the annoying girl, who stayed quiet.

Bar Witch threw her the Man-Hawk's sword. 'If any feathered idiots find their way in, put your aggression to good use. And if you get hungry…' She nodded to the dead Man-Hawks. 'Feast on some feathery meat.'

Bar Witch and Hargon moved barrels off the stones and sealed the room, then walked out into the open.

LORD OF THE LAND

Karl and his friends, their legs and wrists bound by rope, lay on the back of a cart. Karl's head throbbed, and the high sun burned his body.

They travelled through the desert surrounded by forty weary humped horses. Some pulled supply carts while others supported warriors.

Rows of cages followed, stuffed with people wearing rags similar to the tongueless boy and woman.

Karl wanted to cry at the thought. On exiting Barma, the boy and woman were displayed on spikes, their bodies ripped as though a fork had shredded them. Karl thought about the suffering the people must have faced under Lord Lofad's rule and whether things were about to get worse.

Lord Lofad rode three rows ahead, his axe sheathed to his back. He laughed and joked with one of his warriors as though betraying people was normal.

The walls of Jermal dominated the horizon.

Frong looked back at Sags' body, draped over a humped horse, while Marlens stared at her potion belt on another cart along with everyone's weapons.

'Are you okay?' Karl asked Sabrinia.

She stared at the wood of the cart. 'I've failed. This is all my fault.'

'No,' Karl replied. 'You made the best choice you could and did what you thought was right. It just hasn't worked out.' His words echoed his own failings and role in Sags' death. 'You'll never be a failure.'

Sabrinia's lips creased into a faint smile and she raised her bound arms. 'Thanks, but this screams failure.'

Lord Lofad stopped his humped horse and dropped back to them. He grinned. 'Are you having a pleasant journey?'

Sabrinia turned to him. 'Whatever your plan is, I guarantee it's a bad one.'

Lord Lofad chuckled. 'Why risk my life and those of my warriors when I can trade upwards?' He ran his fingers through Sabrinia's hair. 'If these Man-Hawks are as brutal as you say, then your weapons, the offer of my slaves and Arazod's wife will mean I join the winning team and can find this magical relic myself.' He blew his hair out of his face.

Sabrinia's face reddened. 'They'll take what you offer and peck your eyes out! You're an idiot!'

Lord Lofad's jolly expression vanished. He nodded and rejoined his warriors. Lord Lofad's lack of a reaction terrified Karl more than if he had lashed out.

The cart continued until they were alongside Jermal. The sun clipped the top of the walls, at least fifty people high.

While it was majestic, a heavy energy clogged the air.

A shriek pierced Karl's soul. In the arch, a sad ghostly woman lay on her stomach. Her bones poked out of her skin and her ragged crown was so tight a line of dry blood surrounded its rim.

It was as if she were stuck between life and death. Her white pupils with black irises showed an aggressive hunger that contradicted her frail form.

Lord Lofad laughed. He rode his humped horse close to her, stopped and spat through her. She ignored him.

'Hey, look at me!' he said.

She stared towards the back of the group, towards Sags.

Lord Lofad continued to torment the woman, but Karl turned away.

Her eyes burned in Karl's mind and his stomach twisted. He refused to look at her.

'Onwards.' Lord Lofad turned to Sabrinia and Karl. 'We'll stop to rest soon and maybe we'll have some fun with you.'

SOMETHING FISHY

Rings of tents surrounded Karl's cart and the cages of the tongueless.

There was no escape.

Everywhere he turned, the skeletal fish symbol of the Barmashins taunted him.

A fire pit illuminated the night and the heat suffocated everything within range.

Two warriors placed a steel stretcher on branches wedged in the ground and created a cooking platform.

Other warriors drank from pouches and got louder with each sip. They bellowed about Lord Lofad's excellent plan and celebrated their new lives that hadn't started.

Lord Lofad gulped his drink and swirled it in his mouth.

Three warriors dropped to their knees and craned their necks towards their saviour. They opened their mouths like chicks to a mother bird.

Lord Lofad spat the drink into the female warrior's mouth. She swallowed while the other two congratulated her.

Karl wished he'd never met these people. 'On the hopelessness scale where does this sit?' Karl asked Marlens.

'Our weapons are in that tent in the inner ring and we've no chance of gettin' to 'em, so I'd say ultra hopeless.' Marlens shook her head.

Karl would have rather died by Ryza's sword. He turned to Sabrinia. 'I'm sorry, for everything.'

Defeat covered her face. 'Me too.'

He moved his tied wrists and held her hands.

She showed a hint of a smile through the sadness. 'If we get through this, I'll change the laws.'

Karl chuckled. 'Are you just saying that because we're definitely dead?'

She rested her head on his shoulder. 'I think so. But I'd love to be bound to you.'

He kissed the top of her head.

She wiped her nose against the ropes. 'I did read about someone who once unbound two people, so it isn't impossible.'

Frong scratched his beard. 'Vasen, where me and Sags met.' He coughed. 'There were a few situations. People like us would get themselves unbound from former lovers. It was all done in secret though, to avoid punishment.'

Karl pictured his wedding in Flowforn's Great Hall. All of his friends there, watching, but Sags and Larnela weren't. A happy scene drowned in tragedy and blood.

Lord Lofad approached Karl. Two warriors carried a wooden coffin and set it down behind their master. They opened it and calm water rocked back and forth.

Another warrior approached carrying a ceramic vase. She poured hundreds of small fish into the water.

The shredded tongueless boy and woman invaded Karl's mind again.

He turned onto his knees and stared at Lord Lofad. 'Is this how you bathe? It would explain the heavy smell of fish on your hair.'

Lord Lofad smirked. 'We don't need all of you, and you've just volunteered to be the entertainment for our evening meal.' Lord Lofad grabbed Karl by the hair, yanked him onto the mud, and dragged him towards the coffin.

'Leave him!' Sabrinia demanded but a warrior stood in front of her.

Lord Lofad spoke Barmashin with the warrior.

The warrior grabbed Sags' body and dragged him towards the cooking platform.

'No!' Frong protested. He and Marlens flung their bound arms but were met with punches. Frong wept and the sizzling began. He tried to break free, but a warrior held him down.

Lord Lofad booted Karl in the gut and held his head over the fishy coffin.

Karl glanced up at Sabrinia. She swung her bound legs over the side of the cart and hopped off it.

A warrior grabbed her, but she bit him and took a punch. The warrior unsheathed his sword.

'No!' Lord Lofad commanded. He spoke in Barmashin and the warrior growled. Lord Lofad pointed at Sabrinia. 'I'll stop him killing you, but I won't stop him beating you.'

Karl studied Lord Lofad's steel leg. He could try to swipe it and pull him down, but what would that do?

Sabrinia hopped forward. The warrior knocked her to the floor but she got up.

Lord Lofad sighed, pushed Karl onto the mud and kicked him in the stomach. Lord Lofad approached Sabrinia, grabbed her by the throat and slammed her back against the cart. 'Hop back on there.'

Karl spat blood. He knew what she was doing and thought it was a terrible idea. 'Do as he says.'

'No,' Sabrinia replied. 'You need me, Lofad. So I know you can't hurt me.' She smiled.

Lord Lofad pulled on his hair. 'Fine. I'll tell Arazod and his sister that we found you with no legs. And you won't be able to tell the truth, because it seems your tongue left your mouth.' He held his hand out and yelled in Barmashin.

A warrior approached with a dagger and placed it in Lord Lofad's hand.

Sabrinia tried to fight him off but a warrior helped Lord Lofad to hold her still. Sabrinia moved her head out of the way but Lord Lofad grabbed her face and jammed the dagger between her lips and pried it between her teeth.

A warrior yelled some Barmashin.

'What?' Lord Lofad replied. He listened to his warrior and released Sabrinia. 'I'll be back.' He walked towards the outer ring of tents and some warriors followed.

Sags' skin darkened. Marlens held Frong's head against her chest.

Karl thought he hallucinated seeing Peezant again, this time in a tree.

A warrior grunted towards the cages of the tongueless.

A swarm of them burst out of their prison and attacked him. Floods of tongueless overran warriors and entered tents. They savaged any warrior they saw, not caring about their own casualties.

Fists smacked skin and steel sliced flesh.

A grandmotherly tongueless woman nodded at Oaf.

Oaf…

Karl wept, a mixture of hope, happiness, and surprise that fate smiled on them.

Oaf untied Sabrinia and handed her a sword. She cut Marlens and Frong free while Oaf helped Karl to his feet. 'We'll save the hugs for later.'

Frong and Marlens retrieved Sags.

Sabrinia entered the tent and emerged with their weapons. She gave Karl a curved sword and readied her bow and arrow. They battled the warriors, and while they weren't as skilled, they were sober.

A warrior lunged at Oaf. Sabrinia fired an arrow into its back.

Everywhere Karl looked, they were gaining the advantage.

Oaf knocked a warrior out, Karl stabbed another, and Marlens threw a potion into a tent, setting it ablaze.

'Put. Your. Weapons. Down!' Lord Lofad commanded. He held his axe against Questions' throat and approached the coffin of fish.

Karl's eyes widened. The colour drained from Oaf's face.

They all placed their weapons on the ground.

The tongueless elder waved her hand and her people stopped rampaging.

'You've ruined everything!' Lord Lofad said. He drove his elbow into Questions' neck and kicked the back of her knees. He grabbed her hair and held her face above the ravaging water.

Karl wanted to slice Lord Lofad's good leg off.

'You left us no choice,' Sabrinia said. 'Release our friend, and you can go back to Barma and start your life again. We'll pretend we never met, and hopefully we'll never meet again.'

He shook his head. 'I've nothing left.' He pulled Questions' head back.

Karl's heart leapt into his mouth and Oaf lunged forward with no hope of making it, but before Questions became fish food a blade hacked Lord Lofad's good leg. He screamed and fell, holding the back of his knee.

Arazod, frail and wingless, stood above him.

Too many thoughts hammered Karl's brain.

Questions stumbled to Oaf and hugged him.

Arazod grabbed Lord Lofad and pushed him into the fishy coffin. Lord Lofad's screams drowned under thrashing, bloody water. He tried to climb out, but tipped the coffin onto his back. His shredded arms pushed it off and he dragged his torn body across the mud. Fish hung off his ears and the loose flaps of flesh on his back. He stopped at Sabrinia's feet. 'Please...'

Karl wanted her to leave him there.

She kicked him onto his back. 'You don't deserve our mercy, but I'll show you some so I can be sure you're dead.' She took her bow and arrow and shot him through the heart.

Karl charged at Arazod.

Oaf grabbed Karl.

'Let me go, Oaf!' Karl begged.

Oaf pulled him down to the mud and held him. 'There's a lot we need to tell you, Karl.'

Karl had no way out of Oaf's grasp.

The tongueless loaded their dead onto a cart while Oaf explained everything to Karl, from Quizmal being kidnapped to how they found Arazod. Oaf and Questions wept at the news of Sags.

Karl couldn't accept that they had helped Arazod.

'Everything has changed so quickly,' Oaf said.

He was right. From happy and quiet lives they were all broken in some way. Years of peace ruined by a moment of disaster.

Arazod raised a claw to speak.

Karl hated the thought of his voice.

'My sister,' he said weakly. 'She has your Soul of Illuminus.'

Karl's chest tightened.

'And she wants to use it to reawaken Death,' he said.

Frong's head turned from Sags.

Arazod's claws trembled. 'She said she needs something called the Gauntlet of Seliria. It was too cold where Death is—' he wheezed. 'The frosty magic nearly killed us.'

Frong stood. 'We have to find the gauntlet. If she awakens Death then the whole world is hers.'

Karl couldn't get beyond his desire to snap Arazod's neck. He turned to his friends. 'Don't listen to him. He's a liar and will kill us at the first opportunity.'

'He's not with them.' Oaf pointed to Arazod's ruined back.

'This is what he does! He's part of the reason Sags is dead!'

'So are you!' Frong yelled. His face reddened and Karl backed down, flooded with shame and regret.

Silence hung between them all.

Arazod coughed. 'She might already have the gauntlet. But our only chance to beat her is to get ahead.'

Frong nodded. 'It's at least seven sunsets over the southwest sea to Mount Seliria, and those little boats we saw in Barma will get swallowed by the waves.'

Marlens' face sagged.

Frong pulled on his beard. 'The kind of ship we need is underground, in a tunnel that escapes to the sea. Back in Jermal.'

Karl remembered the ghostly woman.

Frong lifted Lord Lofad's dead body and tossed it onto the back of a cart. 'I suggest we gather the dead warriors. We'll need them.'

Karl gathered weapons and water, but there was nothing resembling food.

He mounted a humped horse, wishing he could ride it into Flowforn and that everything would go back to normal. It was as if someone had lifted Hastovia and tossed it against a wall, smashing everything and creating chaos.

Sags, Frong, Marlens and Arazod climbed onto the back of a cart. Marlens treated Arazod's back wounds and Sags' burns. Karl wondered if he was having a nightmare.

Karl pointed his sword at Arazod. 'He needs to be tied.'

Sabrinia remained silent, and Karl was too busy experiencing his own hatred to think about what she must have been feeling. Arazod had ruined her life too. More than that, he had ruined her afterlife.

'Very well.' Arazod held his arms and legs out.

Frong tied rope around Arazod's limbs.

The humped horses started the journey, but Questions refused to get on hers. 'Will I go to Flowforn?'

Oaf climbed down from his creature. 'We have to stay together.'

'Do they need your strength to find the gauntlet?' she asked.

'Well, yes. But we all need each other.'

'Is Quizmal alone?' she asked.

He nodded, crying. 'I'll come with you.' He took her hand but she pulled it away.

'Does he need his ma?' she asked.

'Yes, and his dad,' Oaf said.

'Is it better we split up? Is it better if I fail that you still have a chance? Is it better if you fail that I might help him?'

Oaf's eyes burned with more sadness than Karl had noticed the first time they met.

Questions was right. She couldn't rely on them getting the gauntlet, and she couldn't rely on succeeding her way. So they had to try both, and Oaf increased the chances of securing the gauntlet, not so much sneaking through a castle.

Peezant flew onto Questions' shoulder. 'I can help. Hargon and Bar Witch are in Flowforn,' he squawked.

The silence suggested the decision was made.

'What about you?' Karl asked the tongueless.

They looked at each other and towards their elder. She held her arms out and bowed her head. She and her people turned and left.

'That's gratitude for you,' Karl said.

Oaf squeezed Questions. 'You be careful. I love you.'

'Do I love you too?' she replied.

They kissed. Questions climbed on her humped horse and Karl and Oaf watched her disappear into the forest. Karl placed a hand on Oaf's shoulder. He hoped this wasn't the last time Oaf saw the love of his life.

GHOST TOWN

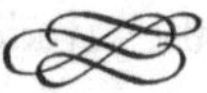

They travelled through the night and the next day, sleeping on their horses and taking turns to lead the pack.

Karl struggled to rest with Arazod nearby. He remembered rescuing Arazod from the Lionbear lair a few years ago, only to be kicked off a cliff as a thank you.

Karl spoke to Oaf to shift his mind. He'd missed him so much and wanted to reassure him they would save his boy, but Oaf was more intent on asking the questions.

'What's it like, killing?' Oaf asked.

Karl felt the weight of Oaf's pain. His people had never killed, but now the darkness of the world tortured him.

'It's horrible,' Karl said. He'd killed a Fool, Man-Hawks and now warriors. 'And those I've killed were at the mercy of someone else. Prisoners in some nonsense cause or greed.'

Oaf nodded and sniffled.

Karl knew if it came to it Oaf would kill for his boy and Questions, but he also knew it would change him forever.

Karl stroked his humped horse's neck. 'My choices were kill or be killed, so I learned to get better at using a sword so I could defend first. I was told a weapon should be used first to prevent death, instead of trying to cause it.'

Frong smiled. 'Like Sags taught you.'

Karl nodded. 'Well, he did say it with a grunt so it really could have been anything.' Sags' face was dry and cracked.

'Good point.' Frong turned to Oaf. 'Weapons only became destructive when the first tribe invaded a castle. It was all shields before, used in battles to knock each other out. There was an unspoken agreement that battles wouldn't be to the death, but rather the loser would be the first knocked unconscious. But when the biggest people kept winning, underhanded tactics and weapons came to be. Then it was a race to see who could invent the most powerful weapons, and battle became more and more attack-based.'

Karl felt a pang of relief. Frong telling a story nobody needed to hear was a sign of progress.

The night sun filled the sky and the walls of Jermal grew on the horizon.

When the group arrived they stood ten or so paces from the arch. That still wasn't far enough for Karl.

The Spirit Queen's shrieking quickened and she stared at the cart of dead bodies. Frong ordered everyone to take only what they needed. They would need to travel light and be prepared to run.

'Why? Why at night?' Karl complained.

Frong stroked Sags' face. 'She's not interested in us,' he told Karl and approached the Spirit Queen. He crouched and met her eyes.

Even though Karl knew she couldn't harm anyone, he feared some power would see her grab Frong and devour him.

'I'm sorry you're in this condition,' Frong said. 'But we need to pass.'

She flashed her crooked teeth at him. He stepped through her and walked onto a narrow bridge that stretched over a man-made drop to a spiky death.

Stone columns and spotless tiles lined the bridge all the way to the perfectly preserved, abandoned, stunning city. Trees boasted vibrant green leaves.

Frong faced Karl. 'The Jermalians didn't always live here. They had an island to themselves, full of trees, fruit, animals and joy.' Frong stepped out of the arch and in front of the Spirit Queen. 'But like with all good things, others got jealous, others wanted, others took.' Frong pulled at his beard. 'You see, the Jermalians were an innovative bunch. They invented the catapult, but used it to fire food across distances before it became a war tool. They also mastered ship structure and taught new farming techniques to those who were stupid. But, rather than see them as forward thinkers and good for Hastovia, some saw their development skills as a threat to their leadership, so as usual, they attacked. They destroyed.'

Karl was fed up of all good things being ruined.

Frong leaned on the wall. 'The queen of Jermal, Tazal, helped her people to escape their island on boats and they washed up far in the north of the Dead Lands.'

Karl's ankles still wore the burn marks from his trip to the Dead Lands.

Frong walked towards Sags and sat on the edge of the cart. He ran his hand over his dead lover's leg. 'But having escaped one kind of death, they suffered from a lack of food and water. It took its toll and Tazal decided she had no choice. Having heard rumours of the Spirit Queen who could grant wishes, she sought her and found her.' He gestured to the wall. 'Tazal wished for a safe home for her people, and the Spirit Queen welcomed her here. As you can see, with only one entrance and these abnormally high walls of magic stone, attacks wouldn't come to Jermal. Plus, who cares about the desert?' He shrugged. 'Jermalians thrived for a while, but what Tazal never knew was that the Spirit Queen fed off the energy of the dead, and as Jermalians naturally passed, she gained more strength, and with that came the power to attack the living. The Spirit Queen wiped them out in a feeding frenzy. But now she is starved again, in a state where she cannot hurt us.'

Sabrinia took a sip of water. 'Isn't she a bit foolish? If she'd let them live she could eat the dead at a normal pace, but by attacking everyone it was basically like burning your own farm down.'

Marlens hopped off the cart and stood by Frong. 'She ate them all for a reason. Wiv enough power, she can break the spell that keeps her on this land. Think of the pain she's feelin'. The god she loved cursed her, and the only way to lift the curse is to kill people. Can't imagine what that does to the old mind.'

'Anyway,' Frong said. 'She will be wanting to eat the dead, so we need to keep her away from Sags. The good thing is we have plenty of distractions.' He tapped the cart full of dead bodies.

'But look how exhausted she is. Can't we carry Sags over her and run?' Karl asked.

Frong shook his head. 'We can't risk it. If there's no ship or she has a burst of energy, Sags will be done.'

Karl understood, but that brought with it a wave of fear.

Frong took a breath. 'The bad thing is we're distracting her by giving her power.' He bit into his beard. 'We'll need to split up. Stay safe.'

FEEDING TIME

arl held Lord Lofad's mutilated corpse above his head and sprinted across the bridge. He took slow breaths and had no idea where he was supposed to go. He refused to look back until Sabrinia called out to him.

He turned. The Spirit Queen could barely drag herself across the bridge.

Sabrinia pointed for Karl to go to his far left. He nodded and glanced at the Spirit Queen. There was something so sad about her. Why would someone curse someone else? There was always some grim trade-off in these old stories.

Karl continued through the impressive city with its white stone buildings – everything perfectly spaced with dwellings all the same size. Trees lined the far wall and all the paths stretched from one end of Jermal to the other.

The castle rose against the back wall and a tower climbed above everything, providing a view of the outside world.

Karl arrived at the far corner. The Spirit Queen had disappeared, which was both reassuring and terrifying. He waited and spotted his friends carrying Sags up the castle steps.

The Spirit Queen crawled through the wall of a house and shrieked. Karl ran back towards Jermal's entrance, luring her away from the others. He took a tiled path that stretched from one wall to the opposite so he could see how far away she was. He waited, staying close enough that she wouldn't shift her focus to Sags.

Karl dumped Lord Lofad's corpse on the tiles and rested his arms. He peered through the window of a house. A sketching of a woman who resembled the Spirit Queen hung on the wall, only she looked happier and beads lined the parchment.

Karl's body chilled. He lifted Lord Lofad and continued along the path until it ended.

Marlens jumped off her cart and threw a body into the far corner. She turned the cart left towards the next corner.

Karl waited for the Spirit Queen and drew her back towards the bridge. Another house displayed a sketching of the Spirit Queen, only there were words under this sketch. 'The Queen of our hearts, Tazal.'

'Tazal?'

Karl's body numbed. The ghostly woman following him wasn't the Spirit Queen, because the Spirit Queen was in front of him and standing. Her swirling red rags covered her grey skin from neck to toe. A mess of scars lived on her bald head and pain stretched her eyes.

She clawed at Karl's face but her bony hands went through him. She shrieked.

Karl dropped Lord Lofad's corpse and ran through Tazal. He turned at the end of the path. The Spirit Queen leaned over Lord Lofad's body and held her hands over his eyes. Black smoke rose from Lofad's eyes and into her fingertips. Lofad's body jerked and crumbled into black smoke.

The Spirit Queen lifted Tazal, flung her away, then floated towards the corpse Marlens had dropped off. Within moments she'd absorbed another soul and body. It wouldn't take long for her to find all the bodies and then, if the stories were true, have the strength to kill Karl and the others.

'Marlens!' Karl called out and ran towards the castle steps.

AN UNWELCOMING HOST

Sabrinia rushed through a tunnel, following Frong who lit the way. She'd left Oaf in the throne room to wait for the others.

Frong placed the jar of light on the ground and lowered Sags down a ledge. Frong took the jar and jumped down.

Sabrinia followed and ran along yet another path. It was the same over and over — run along a path, drop down.

Sabrinia wondered what this place was like in its prosperous days. She passed some Jermalian advancements, like pipework and carts with a wheel mechanism that wouldn't require horses.

The descent continued. Jermalians had perfected defence, as any invaders coming this way would be exhausted by the time they got anywhere near the throne.

Sabrinia hoped she was approaching a ship and not some beast dwelling in the underground.

She caught up with Frong, who placed Sags down in front of a short climb.

'I can hear water,' Frong said.

Arazod caught up.

'Go up and we'll pass him to you,' Sabrinia told Frong.

Frong climbed and Sabrinia and Arazod passed Sags' body up to him.

'Can you help me up, please?' Arazod asked Sabrinia.

He was a helpless wreck, but she couldn't forgive him for forcing her to marry him, for invading her home twice, or for killing Karl's mother. There was only so far her acceptance would stretch. 'Climb up yourself.' She left him and found Frong by the entrance to a cavern.

'Oh Sags… If only you could see this,' Frong said.

Sabrinia stroked Frong's arm.

'Looks like me and Sags might not have been the greatest adventurers.' He chuckled.

The wide cavern opened up in front of Sabrinia and a ship the size of Flowforn castle was tied to steel posts. The setting night sun shone through a distant exit to a river.

Sabrinia thought about jumping into the water and swimming to the ship, but she'd never clear the rocks, so they'd have to take the route of narrow ledges to a path that led to the vessel.

'Run!' Karl shouted from the tunnels.

The accompanying shriek told Sabrinia why.

She ran and jumped down onto the first narrow ledge, worried her aching legs would give in. 'Pass me Sags, then go around me and I'll pass him back,' she told Frong.

Frong passed Sags to Sabrinia. She tensed, worried she'd drop the body.

Frong shuffled past Sabrinia and jumped to the next ledge.

Sabrinia dropped Sags to him and they repeated the move.

Frong jumped down to the last ledge and Sabrinia took Sags in her weakening arms to lower him.

She slipped and grabbed a rock. Sags fell off the side of the ledge and she grabbed his right leg with her other hand.

'Sags!' Frong yelled.

Sabrinia's heart caught in her mouth. Sags was too heavy. Her grip on the rock weakened. Sags was going to become a stain on the rocks. 'I can't!'

The shrieks echoed around them.

Frong reached for Sags but was too far. 'I can't reach! Please hold on, Sabrinia!'

Her fingers slipped along the rock. It was Sags or both of them. 'I'm sorry, Frong.' She let Sags go and closed her eyes. She had failed her friend. 'I'm so sorry.'

'Grab him,' Arazod said.

Sabrinia opened her eyes. Arazod's talons were curved around the platform he hung off. He swung Sags by the ankle until Frong reached out and grabbed his lover's arms. Frong took Sags, leapt onto the path and held him.

Sabrinia pulled Arazod up, his face strained. She felt a moment of sympathy, but it vanished as swiftly as it came. 'Thanks,' she managed.

Arazod nodded and they joined Frong, who continued to the ship and placed Sags on the steps leading below deck. Frong wound in the anchor.

'I'm sorry, Frong,' Sabrinia said.

'You tried.' He looked at Arazod and nodded at him. 'Thank you. Now grab those timber beams.' Frong pointed at the ones on the deck near two of the four ballistas. 'We'll need them to push out of here.' He untied the ropes from the steel posts.

Sabrinia grabbed a beam and pushed off the cave wall.

Frong joined her. 'Arazod, can you steer?'

Arazod nodded and grabbed the wheel.

Another shriek surrounded them.

The ship edged closer to the entrance their friends would emerge from.

'We need to get this ladder up there.' Frong and Sabrinia moved a ladder and placed one end where they came in.

'Come on!' Sabrinia yelled at the tunnel.

Frong held the ladder while she placed a wooden beam on some rocks, ready for the big push. The Jermalians placed strategically flat points among the cavern rocks for this purpose.

Another shriek rippled around the cavern followed by Karl's screams.

INTO THE UNKNOWN

The cold air closed in and nipped at Karl's legs. He spotted the ship and pushed himself.

'There's a ladder!' Sabrinia yelled.

Marlens grabbed it and climbed down, followed by Oaf.

'Hurry!' Frong said.

Karl grabbed the ladder and looked into the tunnels. The Spirit Queen gained on him.

'Go!'

Marlens reached the deck and held the ladder with Frong. The ship moved and the ladder swayed.

'I can't hold it!' Marlens strained.

Oaf fell onto the ship and the ladder headed towards the cavern wall.

Karl dropped a few rungs and held on, but it smashed against the rocks and he splashed into the water.

'Grab the rope!' Frong tossed him some rope and Karl grabbed it. Frong pulled him along as the ship edged towards the mouth of the cavern.

Karl pulled himself to the ship, climbed up and rolled onto the deck. He pulled the rope out of the water and thanked Frong.

Oaf picked up a timber beam while Marlens joined Arazod.

'Push harder!' Frong yelled. He grabbed a timber beam.

The Spirit Queen flew out of the tunnel and turned towards them. They were close to the exit, but the ship scraped against the wall and stopped.

'Push!' Frong said.

Karl sprinted for a ballista. 'If she's had enough souls to attack us, maybe it means we can attack her.' He lifted a heavy, steel arrow. 'Does anyone know how to use this?'

'I do.' Marlens ran over and helped him. 'You turn the winch to stretch the drawstring back.' They loaded the arrow into the trough, cinched it and fired. The arrow flew towards the Spirit Queen.

A flick of her wrist knocked it away.

Frong's mouth fell open.

Karl turned to Marlens. 'On the hopelessness scale?'

'I'm going to say astonishingly hopeless,' Marlens said.

Oaf pressed his hands against the wall and pushed the ship off.

Karl had to buy them time to gather speed. 'All of you get to the front of the ship.' He grabbed the rope, secured it to his waist and tied one end to the mast. He stood at the stern trembling. He drew his curved sword.

'What are you doing?' Sabrinia yelled.

Maybe he was being stupid, but there was no way the ghoul was getting to Sags.

The sunrise caught the front of the ship as they exited the tunnel. 'Drop the sails, quick!' Frong commanded.

The demon slowed.

Karl turned to his friends. 'We're going to make it,' he smiled

'Karl!' Marlens shouted.

The Spirit Queen's legs wrapped around Karl's waist. She pushed him face first onto the deck.

He thrashed his arms around, but she pulled his head back

and placed her grey hands over his eyes. The smell of her rotten skin filled his nostrils and he retched.

Karl's body jerked and something behind his eyeballs ripped. His vision blurred into black and his body temperature dropped. His friends' screams faded until his head filled with the pained cries of hundreds of voices. They grew louder and louder and then the Spirit Queen shrieked.

The voices died and Karl's brain burned into nothingness.

BLUE BLUES

Everything was dark. Karl couldn't open his eyes but an image formed in them, the faint outline of mountains.

'Life is death,' a strained voice said. The words weren't coming from Illuminus.

'Life is death.' It sounded like his mother, Larnela.

'Life is death.' Was that Sags?

The words repeated.

It took him a moment to remember what had happened. Something was missing; the Spirit Queen had taken it. Cold air filled his heart.

Illuminus' face appeared from the dark and tried to consume him, shocking him alert.

He woke up on a swaying bed in a wooden room.

Potion bottles covered the floor. Marlens sat at the foot of his bed.

Her tired eyes shone. 'You made it back!'

'Marlens…' He smiled and tried to sit up but his bare chest tightened. He touched his face. 'What happened? I felt my life slip away.'

Marlens nodded. 'It did a bit, it seems. But we got to the end of Jermal just before the ghost lunatic could finish whatever the weird eye smoke sucking thing she was doin' was.'

Karl's muscles ached.

Marlens handed him a cup of green liquid. 'It tastes of feet but'll help your muscles recover.'

He drank it and the description was fair. 'What is this?' He let it sit in his mouth before experiencing the rancid taste again.

'It's bacteria from Flowforn stream.'

That didn't seem like the worst thing.

'Mixed with powdered horned wolf dung.'

Karl's face dropped.

'I'm messing.' Marlens chuckled. 'Or am I?'

Karl swallowed and smiled. 'How long have I been like this?'

'Two sunsets.'

'What?' It seemed like a moment. A scary, confusing moment. 'Is everyone else okay?'

Marlens nodded and lifted an empty jar. 'I tried about twenty different mixtures to get you to wake up, and you know what worked in the end? The old-fashioned technique of shoving garlic up your nose.' She placed her hand on his forearm. 'We were really worried about you.'

Karl nodded. 'Where's Sabrinia?'

'She's having a snooze. Let's head up. They'll wanna see you, then maybe she'll have woken up.'

The night sun shone on the ship's deck. Water flowed around them for as far as Karl could see and the breeze cooled his skin.

Frong's arms wrapped around Karl from behind. 'It's really you.'

Karl patted Frong's wrists. 'I think so.'

Frong released him and they shared a proper hug. 'I was so worried. You kept making strained noises, but your breaths were so slow.'

Karl pulled away from the hug. 'I'm not going anywhere until we get Sags back.'

Frong smiled. 'We have a lot to catch up on, but for now I should probably steer the ship.' Frong laughed and returned to his captain duties.

'Has he been trouble?' Karl asked Marlens about Arazod, who lay by the mast.

Marlens shook her head. 'He just likes to lie out here and feel the wind on his feathers.'

'Well, I'll stay up here and watch him,' Karl said.

Marlens shrugged. 'Whatever you want. This ship is incredible. They kitted it out like they'd have to live on it a while. We got loads of water, and all the salt seeds in Hastovia.' She offered him some.

He heaved them into his mouth. 'Thanks. Can I ask you something?'

She nodded.

He gestured for them to walk to the stern. They were a world away from home. He took a breath and stared at Marlens' friendly face. 'Do you hate me?'

Even in the dark her face flushed.

Karl chuckled. 'You've never been good at hiding it. It's okay, though, I'll hate me forever if we don't get him back.'

She shook her head. 'I did hate you. Of course I did. Then we nearly lost you and the hatred left. Our moments could all end in a flash and I have no time for hate. And it made me think. Sags made his choice. You didn't stick the sword through him and I know I would've done exactly the same thing as you if I had a chance to resurrect the dead.'

'Thanks.' Karl smiled. 'Who would you have brought back?'

Marlens scratched her nose and seemed uncomfortable. 'Just someone I used to love who didn't love me back.'

Karl nodded. Marlens had never shared much about her past.

She leaned back on the wood. 'Even if he wouldn't ever love me, I wanna give him another chance at life. He was gone young.

So, yeah, I know it all went a bit wrong, but we can only do what we're doing now, so best to get on wiv it.'

He was thankful to count such a kind person among his friends.

They joined Frong, the embodiment of determination, focused on the sea in front of them.

'Want me to take over?' Karl asked. 'I've no idea what I'd be doing but I get the feeling you haven't slept much.'

Frong chuckled. 'I'm fine. It makes the sunsets go faster.'

Karl reached into the bucket of seeds by Frong and offered him some.

Frong opened his mouth and Karl poured them in.

'I was thinking,' Karl said. 'If Illuminus is out of our reach, are there other ways to bring someone back from the… not being alive?'

Frong nodded. 'There's the Heart of Hastovia you saw before.'

Karl remembered the tree that granted wishes on days when beings weren't cruel to each other. 'But it's a lifetime or so away from granting another wish.'

The wind blew stronger.

Frong tucked his beard into his shirt. 'There are probably things we haven't discovered, and there is alchemy that can do it, but the only alchemist to ever resurrect another vanished.'

'Pagar,' Marlens said. 'He was the most powerful alchemist, but when he disappeared so did his knowledge of the alchemist clan that educated him. You see, a lot of potion making, it all comes from emotion.' She looked down. 'I failed Sags because I was scared.'

Karl offered her a reassuring smile. 'You prolonged his life. You gave him a chance to say goodbye.'

'Karl,' Arazod's whiny voice said. 'I'm sorry.'

Karl turned to the broken Man-Hawk. 'You don't get to talk to me.' Karl barged past him and returned to the stern of the ship. The cold air in his heart filled with anger, and the thoughts running through his mind scared him. He didn't want to kill Arazod; he wanted to torture him. Karl remembered when he'd pushed the Soul Bleeder into Arazod's back as a warning. Back then he had the strength to stop, but now... no. There was darkness in him and it grew and he'd dig the axe deeper until it cut through Arazod. People forgave simple things like stealing a meal, burning someone's clothes, or accidentally losing a pet. For killing someone's mother, though? There was no forgiveness for that; only revenge.

Marlens approached Karl. 'You don't have to be his friend, but we all need each other right now.'

'What need do we have for a flightless bird?' Karl said loud enough for Arazod to hear. 'We should chuck him overboard.'

Marlens shook her head. 'His wounds are the sort that don't just stay on the surface.'

Karl didn't care. 'I'm sorry, Marlens. I see nothing but lies with him. He is pure evil, and that doesn't disappear under suffering, it just waits, gathering energy until it's ready to attack again.'

Marlens pulled on her hair. 'Have you never had a dark thought?' She pointed to Arazod. 'He never had no one to stop him actin' on them.'

It wasn't the time for kindness. 'I'm going back to bed.' Karl went below deck to distract himself.

There were so many rooms, made for over a hundred people. The warm orange-brown colour of the wood was the same as a chest of drawers in Karl's old room. It comforted him.

There were rooms for entertainment, with targets for bow and arrow practice, dummies to strike, and card tables. Three large dining halls boasted shelves stocked full of herbs, soaked beans, seeds and for some reason jars upon jars of powdered garlic.

Karl entered a weapons room, took a steel sword and sheathed it. He passed by worship rooms and baths.

If they didn't have a mission they could live on this ship for years.

A map of Hastovia covered a wall. Jermalians had marked the places they knew of.

Their old home was a small island to the northeast of the Dead Lands, and Flowfornia was simply a small part of a giant world. Larger islands existed far to the north and even in the direction they were headed, while the far east was all sea, seemingly unexplored. Karl wanted to explore more of the world. He wondered if there were places untouched by conflict and horror.

He turned from the map and entered a tiled bathroom. Sags lay in a bath with sacks of sand tied to his feet and wrists to keep his body submerged. At least under there the insects couldn't get to him.

Karl sat on the edge of the bath. Sags' dark skin had more blisters and was looser. Karl bit his bottom lip and cried. 'I'm sorry, Sags.' He imagined them training and running around the castle grounds to keep fit. Sags always made Karl feel as if he could be special, even if he only communicated through grunts for most of their friendship. If anything, only being able to communicate through looks, gestures and grunts made their bond more honest. It was all in the eyes – no words to hide behind. Sags was a presence that inspired and gave people energy. Karl only had to think of the love Frong and Marlens felt for him. Karl smiled through the tears. 'I can't wait until you're back.'

Karl turned to leave but Sabrinia stood there, crying. 'I saw this black stuff come out of your eyes. I thought you'd never wake up.' She threw her arms around him.

Karl took her hands. 'I'm sorry. I had to stop her getting to Sags.'

She nodded. 'I know. Just for now... be quiet.'

She pressed her lips to his. Karl's heart lightened. Maybe things would work out and life could return to normal.

They returned to Sabrinia's room and tore each other's clothes off, releasing the tension of all that had gone on. They lay in each other's arms, hot and happy. The silence didn't need filling; it was beautiful. Karl turned to sleep, but feared these moments would end when they got to their destination.

The sunsets passed without incident. The endless blue rolled on and became more boring than majestic. Were they even getting anywhere?

Frong assured Karl they were making progress and pointed out the movement of the stars when the night sun rose. Karl didn't see any change but trusted him anyway.

Karl lay on the deck with Sabrinia and stared at the night sun.

Frong laughed in the face of choppy waters and ocean spray battering his face. The adventurous spirit Karl knew him for had returned.

Sabrinia turned to Karl. 'Do you wish we could just stop?'

His fingers brushed hers. 'Stop what?'

'Everything. Go and live in a cave somewhere. Leave the needs of others behind.'

Karl nodded. 'Have you been guzzling the ale?'

She chuckled. 'No. I just want to imagine a different path sometimes.'

'Well, yes. Of course. I'd love to do that. But we are the way we are and who we are. And we feel the way we do about each other because of our stupid impulsive need to help.' He imagined them in a cave deep in a forest, surrounded by animals that didn't want to eat them. 'You'd get bored of me after a few sunsets, find a village and start building people huts or scrubbing their children.'

She laughed. 'I think you're right.' She kissed his cheek. 'I'm going to train.' She got up and walked below deck.

Oaf and Arazod gazed at the ocean.

'I… I'm sorry… for my part in what Lord Ragnus did to your people,' Arazod said.

Oaf nodded. 'I'll never forget or forgive what you did. But I'm glad you've seen that what you did was wrong.'

Arazod nodded. 'I don't expect you to forgive me. I just wanted you to know—' he wheezed. 'I am sorry. And I'm grateful for your kindness.'

Oaf folded his arms. 'Why do you conquer?'

Karl wished he could be like Oaf, always trying to understand.

Arazod shook water off his feathers. 'It's just how we are raised. My father was betrayed once—' he wheezed. 'And to stop ever being betrayed again, he decided the best thing to do would be to become the most powerful being in Hastovia. Power is security.'

Karl wanted to say something snide, but shifted his focus to the stars.

Oaf scratched his head. 'But isn't that something you can't get? There's no limit to power. It's a dumb goal.'

Arazod shrugged. 'I don't have an argument against that—' he coughed. 'Where I grew up, we didn't get to choose.'

Karl could get up, take a few steps and jam his sword into Arazod's spine. It would be easy.

His mother bled in his arms all over again. Karl stood and stepped towards Arazod, his hand on his sword handle. One movement is all it would take.

His grip tightened around the handle, but he stopped himself. It would be better they use Arazod to get what they need and throw him to any monster they might encounter.

Karl turned back and removed his hand from his sword handle. The ship tipped and Karl slammed against the deck.

'What in Hastovia is that?' Frong yelled.

A WORLD OF ITS OWN

demonic rock spiral burst out of the sea like a stone tail reaching for the clouds.

Frong swerved the ship around it and another rock spiral shot out of the blue.

Sabrinia emerged from below deck and her eyes widened.

Karl pushed himself onto his feet. Over the edge of the ship, small blue circular shadows the size of his head appeared. 'Erm… what are the weird little blue circles?'

'What blue circles?' Frong swerved away from another rock spiral.

'There are more over here,' Arazod said from the opposite side of the ship.

The shadows broke through the water. Blue, scaly, muscular people with sharp teeth and holes where their noses should be rode large grey-scaled, yellow-finned sharks with glowing tentacles.

Karl thought he'd be safe on the ship, but the sharks leapt high enough for the blue people to hop onto the deck

'Turn your ship around!' one of them commanded.

Karl unsheathed his sword and raised his shield. 'You should turn around and get back on your… shark thing.'

The creature leapt at Karl, who bashed it into Oaf.

Oaf grabbed the creature and threw it into the ocean.

Another blue thing jumped at Sabrinia, who shot an arrow into its shoulder.

Arazod kicked a creature that tried to climb aboard, while Marlens protected Frong.

Each time a creature invaded, it was repelled, but they wouldn't be able to keep it up. The creatures kept coming and they forced the group back towards Frong.

'Turn your ship around!' the creature commanded again.

'We have to keep going that way.' Karl pointed at the endless blue.

The scales on the creature's forearms opened and a spike grew out of a hole. 'Then you will die.' The creatures edged forwards.

The boat tipped sideways, throwing them off balance, but it wasn't enough.

Karl placed his sword and shield by his feet and raised his hands, hoping to avoid any bloodshed. 'Please. Just let us get on with our journey.'

The creature retracted its spike and all the blue beings leapt off the ship.

Karl and Oaf exchanged a confused glance.

'So I guess sometimes all we need to do is be polite.' Karl shrugged.

'I don't think manners had anything to do with it,' Frong said.

Karl turned around. 'Oh.'

A grey, slimy round sheet twice the size of the ship moved through the water. Eight barbed tentacles stretched out around it.

'I hope my eyes are toying with me,' Karl said.

'If they are, mine are doing the same,' Oaf replied.

Frong swung the ship around to avoid whatever it was and it moved in the opposite direction.

Its tentacles shot around to point at the ship and it sped towards them.

'Hold on, everyone,' Frong said.

The creature's tentacles slapped the side of the vessel as though trying to figure out what it was.

Marlens took a jar from her belt. 'Let's try something.' She opened the jar, poured its contents into another and threw it as far as she could. 'Cover your ears.'

The jar exploded into a plume of smoke.

The tentacles turned and the sheet moved to the smoke.

'I reckon those tentacles feel for movement,' Marlens said.

A tentacle rose up to the sky and its tip pointed towards the ship.

Marlens put her finger to her lips. The tentacle lowered and she whispered. 'I reckon it can hear with them too.'

Karl nodded and whispered back. 'But how do we avoid it when we're in a moving vessel?'

She shrugged. 'Let's just stay quiet. It might go away.'

The others all stood at the back of the ship. Beyond the tentacles, the blue creatures waited on their shark mounts.

The tentacles stroked the water's surface and one by one they pointed towards the ship, but this time the sheet moved slower until it was next to them.

Karl held his breath.

Marlens took another jar and whispered. 'I don't have enough of these, so we have a choice. Keep distracting it and hope it gets bored, or go for the kill.'

They agreed. Marlens mixed the potions, tossed them onto the grey sheet and pointed for everyone to drop to the deck.

Karl hit the deck and hoped.

'Frong, turn!' Marlens yelled.

The ship swerved and an explosion rocked it.

Karl slid to the far side of the vessel. When it settled, he stood and inspected the damage.

The smoke cleared and he smiled. 'You did it, Marlens!'

Sabrinia pointed into the distance. 'I guess it's their cue to come back.' The blue creatures approached again.

Karl readied his sword and shield.

A jet of water sprayed from the sea and covered everyone. A wave knocked the ship.

Karl's heart battered his chest.

The grey sheet and barbed tentacles rose out of the blue. Like a slimy veil, it hung over the head of an armless giant with tusks and no eyes. Thousands of holes covered its face like stab wounds, and sea snakes fell out of them.

A tentacle swiped a blue creature along with its shark and tossed them into the beast's toothless mouth.

Three tentacles grabbed the side of the ship and pulled the vessel towards the monster.

Sea snakes dropped to the deck and Karl whacked and sliced them.

Frong thrust his spear at a tentacle, but it dodged and wrapped around his chest.

Karl dropped his sword, lunged and grabbed Frong's leg. He was in a tug of war with an opponent he could never beat.

'Hold on!' Marlens helped Karl, but it made no difference.

Sabrinia's arrows stuck in the creature's face, but a tentacle whipped her across her head.

'Sabrinia!' Karl yelled. She was out cold.

The tentacle yanked Frong out of Karl and Marlens' grasp and pulled Frong towards its mouth.

Karl reached for his sword but it was gone.

Arazod had it. He jumped onto a tentacle, ran up to the creature's shoulder and hacked at the tentacle holding Frong.

Frong dropped into the sea among the sea snakes.

Another tentacle swiped Arazod and raised him above the sea beast's mouth.

Marlens tied several potion bottles around a ballista bolt. 'Karl, quick!'

Karl took aim. He hesitated for a moment. He could let Arazod die and then fire the bolt.

'Karl!' Marlens yelled.

Arazod dangled, screaming, swiping the sword at nothing.

Karl fired and pierced the monster's shoulder, setting it alight.

It roared and smashed Arazod against the sea. It retreated to the underwater world and the ocean rose and fell. Arazod, Frong and the bodies of the blue creatures vanished into the deep.

SEA, SEA, SEE

$\mathcal{A}$razod coughed and dug his claws into the tentacle wrapped around his throat, hoping to free himself before it pulled him under the water again.

Every breath crushed his chest and felt as if it could burst his lungs.

He raked the tentacle.

'Stop scratching me!' Karl said.

Arazod gripped the tentacle and realised it was an arm. The water around them was still and Arazod stared at the sky.

Karl tied a rope around Arazod's chest and Oaf pulled him back onto the ship.

Arazod collapsed onto the wooden deck.

Sabrinia ran towards Karl as he climbed onto the ship.

Nobody had ever worried for Arazod nor feared for his safety.

Marlens knelt by Arazod and rubbed green powder into his feathers. He had no idea what it was but it made the gash less painful. She was impressive. How different things could've been in the past if someone like her was on his side.

'You okay?' Marlens asked.

He nodded, struggling to form words without pain.

'Thanks, Karl,' Arazod said.

Karl stared at him with less hatred, but the hatred was still there and he knew he deserved it. Karl would never forgive him, but he didn't want his forgiveness. He only wanted to feel that he could exist without having to worry about a sword ramming through the back of his neck.

Karl approached Arazod and offered him a handful of salt seeds.

Arazod's hands trembled and he accepted them. He tossed them into his beak and nodded appreciation.

'Thanks for saving Frong,' Karl said.

Frong squeezed water out of his shirt, extended his hand and pulled Arazod up to his feet. 'It's appreciated, Arazod.'

It was strange. They weren't offering him their obedience, but they were being respectful, and it wasn't through fear or force.

Karl turned to Frong. 'What was that thing? A god?'

Frong shook his head. 'I've no idea. It's the biggest creature I've ever seen and compares to nothing I've heard described. We're in a part of the world we don't know much about now.'

'Might be time for a fourth edition of that book,' Karl said.

'Look,' Marlens said.

The blue creatures rode their fish, far behind them now.

If they tried to attack again, Arazod would stick his talons through their faces, but the distance grew until they disappeared. It seemed they knew what was best for them.

Oaf handed Arazod a drying sheet.

'Thank you.' Arazod admired Oaf. He had the strength to bash most beings, but didn't flaunt it. He treated Arazod like a being, nothing else. Oaf was honest about his feelings and it didn't matter that Arazod was a Man-Hawk, or a Man-Hawk without wings. To Oaf he was someone to try to find common ground with. Even as an enemy. It was bizarre but he appreciated it.

Arazod felt his strength return and he had this group of people, a group of people he had ruined the lives of, to thank.

'No time to rest,' Frong said.

Karl nodded. 'Yep. Just as I imagined. It looks like somewhere I wish we didn't have to go.'

There it was on an island, halfway up a mountain. The door to the castle within the rocks. In there was the power his sister craved. A power that could save or destroy the world.

FREE THE PEOPLE

lowfornians chomped down fruit as though they'd never eaten. Bar Witch would have to eat hay if they continued eating at this pace.

'It's great, isn't it?' Hargon fed the baby some berries.

'What? It's disgraceful,' Bar Witch answered.

He shook his head. 'Sure they could treat the food like it needs to last a bit longer, but they're smiling, and we caused that.'

He had a point, but there was a bigger concern. 'We can't keep going in and out to get food, though.'

Hargon huffed. 'True. And other Man-Hawks might decide to search the tavern.'

Bar Witch raised a hand. 'Listen! Oi, idiots!' She had their attention. 'You lot eating like vultures isn't something that'll see us live very long, so it's time to escape.'

They stared at her.

'But we have to go one by one, so me and Hargon can lead you safely. Then, when you're in the woods, you go to the lake and wait for others. Got it?'

They stared at her.

She sighed. 'Who's coming first?'

An old man, Grolt, raised his arm.

Hargon handed the baby to a Flowfornian man. 'I'll get into position.' He left.

Bar Witch walked Grolt to the tavern entrance and looked out at Flowforn.

Hargon waited, crouched by a boulder.

'Okay,' Bar Witch said. 'First you go to that statue of King Sastin and wait while the flying idiot above does his circle. Then when I raise my right fist, you make a break for it. Got it?'

'Yes,' Grolt said.

'Once you get to Hargon, squeeze behind that boulder and there's a gap in the wall that'll get you outside.'

Grolt nodded. 'Thank you.'

'Good luck.' Bar Witch waited for the Man-Hawk patrolling the skies to fly towards the opposite wall. 'Go.'

Grolt sprinted to the statue and sat against it. Bar Witch gave him a thumbs up. This would be easy. Now they needed to wait. The Man-Hawk flew above them and would be gone any moment.

He flew down instead and stood by the well, close to the statue.

Grolt stared at Bar Witch.

It would be fine. She raised a finger for him to wait.

He buried his head in his knees.

Another Man-Hawk landed next to the other and they spoke.

Bar Witch didn't know what to do. The longer she left Grolt, the higher the risk. She had to do something. Why was this all on her?

She waited until the Man-Hawks stepped away. She raised her right fist and Grolt ran, but the Man-Hawks turned and spotted him.

'Stop!' one said.

Hargon ducked behind the boulder.

Grolt raised his arms.

The Man-Hawks flew in front of him. 'What are you doing?'

Bar Witch held her breath.

'Nothing,' Grolt said.

'This is your last chance to say something useful,' the Man-Hawk said.

Bar Witch needed to do something, but if she did they'd both be dead, and more people needed her. Is this what being a leader was – sacrificing people?

Grolt spat in the Man-Hawk's face. A sword pierced Grolt's stomach.

Bar Witch hated herself.

A HELPING HAND

The steel door, midway up the mountain was unnecessarily big, unless it was for giants, in which case it was terrifying. A line ran through a hand-shaped mould and all the way up the door to a small, dull crystal.

Oaf pounded the door. 'How are we supposed to get in? I can't even beat it down.'

Frong pointed to the crystal. 'It's a guardian stone. And I guess this hand mould is a mechanism to operate it.' He placed his hand in the mould but nothing happened. 'It seems this was protected with magic so Seliria was the only one who could get in or out.'

'So there's no way in for us?' Karl glanced at their ship, anchored at the bottom of the mountain. They'd left Sags in his bath, the best place for him.

Karl wondered if they'd wasted all those sunsets. He wished they'd let him sneak into the castle to retrieve the orb.

'Well, we could try fire,' Frong said. 'Her gauntlet allowed her to command flame so it would make sense that her flaming hand got her in. Marlens?'

Marlens grabbed the orange jar from her belt. 'Give me your spear,' she asked Frong.

He handed it over and she poured the orange liquid on it, setting it ablaze. She rubbed the spearhead into the mould of the hand. Fire burned on the steel, but nothing happened. 'Nope...' She clipped the jar back to the belt.

Karl rubbed his finger along scratches on the side of the door. 'Looks like someone's already tried to get in.'

Arazod nodded. 'Man-Hawks...'

Frong scratched his beard. 'Then they've already been here and failed.'

'She'll be back,' Arazod said. 'She'll find a way. When she wants something, she obsesses. If she can't get the gauntlet she'll find another route to Death—' he wheezed. 'It will likely involve a lot of lives ending.' Arazod climbed on top of a rock and shrieked.

'What are you doing?' Oaf asked.

'If Man-Hawks are still here they will come and we can fight them and get answers.'

The last thing Karl wanted was more Man-Hawks.

'There.' Arazod pointed to the remains of a fire.

They all ran over.

'Feathers and blood,' Sabrinia said.

Karl grabbed Marlens and gestured for her to follow him.

'Marlens, I need to set my hand ablaze and put it in that mould.'

She looked at him as though he was mad. 'Your hand'll cook. No chance.'

'We need the gauntlet,' Karl said. 'We can't risk her getting it. I'd give up all my limbs for Sags, so just help me out.'

She bit her lip.

'Please. If it burns to a crisp we can use the wizard-lizard hair to get me it back.'

Marlens shook her head.

'Can you think of a better way?' he asked.

She rubbed her chest and grimaced. 'Put your hand out, then.'

He did and she rubbed red lotion onto it. 'This won't save your hand, but it'll make it less horrible. But that ain't saying much.'

Karl took a breath. 'Thank you.' He grabbed the bottle of orange liquid from her and poured a semi-circle around the door to prevent anyone stopping him. The flames rose.

Karl kissed his hand goodbye. 'See you soon.'

'You only need a few drops.' Marlens winced.

Karl nodded. He hesitated and looked away. For Sags.

He poured the orange liquid on his left hand until it was covered in flame. He jammed it into the mould.

'I'm going to need to look away,' Marlens said.

Karl stared at his hand, fascinated by the movement of flames around his fingers.

The mould shifted around his hand and fire ate his fingertips. The mould locked onto his wrist and he couldn't move.

He tried to fight the agony but he screamed and the others rushed towards him, stopped by the flames.

'What are you doing?' Sabrinia yelled.

'Sorry,' Marlens said.

'Put the fire out!' Sabrinia demanded.

'Don't do it!' Karl yelled.

Sweat covered his face and his head swayed. Sharp pain consumed his hand and his wrist burned and blistered. An orange glow filled the line towards the gem and it turned amber.

The door clicked, the mould released Karl's hand and the door slid down into the ground.

Marlens pulled Karl away from the door and threw some black powder over his hand, extinguishing the flames.

Karl faded and caught a glimpse of a shadow high up the mountain.

Arazod shrieked again.

STEELY SECRETS

'Karl! Karl!' Sabrinia tapped his face, but he wouldn't move. 'How could you let him?' she yelled at Marlens, who rubbed swamp vine into Karl's gums.

'He just needs rest,' Marlens said.

'Look at his hand!' Bones poked out of Karl's blistered, red-raw mess. 'Is this your revenge for Sags?'

Marlens stared at Sabrinia but said nothing.

Oaf pulled Sabrinia from the cold steel room they stood in. 'Karl wanted this. It's not her fault.'

Oaf was right, but Marlens should have stopped him. Karl wasn't thinking straight.

Frong stepped outside of the room. 'It might be wise to split up. We should leave Marlens to help Karl while we get the gauntlet.'

Sabrinia nodded. She entered the room, touched Karl's face and kissed his forehead. 'We'll be back soon.'

Sabrinia should've apologised to Marlens but decided against it and rejoined the others. 'Where do we start?'

'We find the throne room.' Frong scanned the room. 'Where's Arazod?'

Arazod shrieked. He emerged from a steel chamber.

Hundreds of steel rooms, connected by steel lines, sat within the rocks.

'I was investigating,' Arazod said. 'What are these? Rooms for warriors?'

Frong shook his head. 'These are steel chambers of death.' He pointed to ashen stains on the steel floor. 'Stories tell of people being imprisoned here. Seliria would heat this entire place, the furnace spreading through those steel lines, until her prisoners burned.'

Acid rose in Sabrinia's throat. They stood on a mass murder site.

Frong scratched his beard. 'I heard her downfall came because she wasn't selective about who she imprisoned. Some heroes had themselves deliberately arrested, then burst out of their cells.' He pointed to a room with the door blown off. 'And they killed her. Thankfully.'

'This place is creepy,' Oaf said.

Sabrinia took an arrow from her quiver. Steel lines connected each hall and room, so even in a peaceful dining hall, Seliria's flaming touch could reach anyone. It wasn't so much the torturous surroundings that made Sabrinia uneasy, but the silence of murder, the freezing emptiness, and the smell of ash that even after years of inactivity still lingered like souls trapped.

They entered the throne room, lined with steel carvings of a horned creature of fire, riding the wind.

'This place is a monument to her obsession with Pyralus,' Frong said.

A glass bridge stretched over rocky pits packed with charred skeletons.

Sabrinia crossed the bridge and walked over an ash-covered grate. Chains hung above it. 'I hope that isn't what I think it is.'

Frong nodded. 'Seliria loved watching.'

Sabrinia continued to Seliria's circular steel throne and

studied it. All the steel lines flowed out of it and into the rocky walls like a web. From here Seliria could control the heat in her entire kingdom.

Sabrinia's head shot to the far corner. 'Anyone see that?'

Holes dotted the ceiling.

'It's nothing,' Frong said. 'It's normal to hear noises and see things where there are none. It's part of being in spooky settings. The mind plays all sorts of tricks.'

'Let's get the gauntlet and get out of here,' Oaf said.

Sabrinia walked to a door where stairs descended into darkness. 'Hopefully it's down here, and that's all that's down here.'

Arazod tapped her shoulder.

Sabrinia shuddered. She'd never get used to him being on their side.

'What do you plan to do when you get the gauntlet?' he asked.

'I think it would be wise to destroy it,' Frong said. 'Then nobody will be able to awaken Death or command fire. The existence of such power is enough to motivate evil, so it's best to be rid of it.'

Oaf looked at the ground.

'Or we use it to kill Ryza,' Arazod suggested.

'That's dangerous, though,' Oaf said. 'If it goes wrong she has it, then she'll have no reason to keep Quizmal around.' He clenched his fists. 'And what if she offers us a swap? Quizmal for the gauntlet?'

'Pointless,' Arazod said. 'As soon as she has the gauntlet she'd fry us so you'd—' he wheezed. 'Get a hug before being cooked with your son.'

Sabrinia sat on Seliria's throne, imagining the pain she had caused from it.

Arazod wheezed. 'We should use it and have it on our side. No evil will approach if there's the threat of being burned to death.'

Frong chuckled. 'We both know that's not true. The seduction of power draws evil towards it.' He scratched his beard. 'If you knew this power existed in a castle somewhere, you and your Fools and Lord Ragnus would have been upon it swiftly.'

Arazod nodded. 'It is an attractive power to have.'

Sabrinia tapped her arrow against the steel armrest. 'Like Oaf said, there's a risk we lose and Ryza takes the gauntlet.'

'The reward of her dying is worth it,' Arazod argued.

Sabrinia nodded. 'Then we have a plan. We use it to destroy Ryza, and then we destroy the gauntlet. This isn't a power that should exist.'

'But it can help to keep order in the world,' Arazod pushed.

'We have our plan. And I'll be the one to kill Ryza with it,' Sabrinia said.

A flood of gangly and grey half-human, half-deer creatures climbed out of the holes in the walls.

'Maybe we should get going,' Oaf said.

Frong's eyes widened. 'Gygus are meant to be extinct.'

'Looks like they're far from it,' Sabrinia said.

The group turned and ran, leaving the grunts of the Gygus behind.

A WORTHY LEADER

'He died because of me, because I rushed it. I could've waited more.' Bar Witch placed a handful of berries on an abandoned cart.

'It's not your fault. We watched the Man-Hawks patrol and we were unfortunate they changed their movements,' Hargon said.

'I'm not supposed to be responsible for morons. Drinks I brew. Idiots I amuse. But caring for lives, that's not me and it shows.' Grolt might have been old but he had more life in him than most Flowfornians who spent time in the tavern. Bar Witch was responsible for him and she let him die.

Hargon scratched a circle into the bark of a tree. 'You've been amazing. And nothing we do is without risk, even this. We're risking our lives now for what? So people who might escape have enough food and a safe path that might not even end up safe.' He carved a circle into another tree.

'I'm not going back. They're all yours,' she said.

'I need you, Bar Witch,' Hargon said.

Bar Witch kicked the wheel of the cart. 'They're better off hiding in that room until someone rescues them.'

'Or until they get found and enslaved or slaughtered?' Hargon folded his arms.

He was right.

'Don't care. I'm done.' She walked away.

'Grolt put his hope in you because he trusted you. Even at the end he stayed loyal to what we're doing, because he believed we have a chance. And so do I. I know behind that moody attitude you care, so feel free to disappear and start a new life, but this'll always be in your head. You'll always wonder if you did the right thing,' Hargon said.

She could walk until she found a port and she could disappear to a far-flung island in Hastovia. But it would be all she'd ever think about. She turned to him. 'Moody attitude?'

'Sorry. Alternative attitude?' He shrugged.

She chuckled.

'We can do this, but only if we do it together,' Hargon said.

Bar Witch nodded, but had no idea how they'd succeed. 'Let's get more berries.'

'What do you think makes a good leader?' Hargon picked berries and threw them onto the cart. 'Is it being selfless, being kind, or being like Arazod and basically being insane?'

'No idea. Telling others what to do?' Bar Witch suggested. 'What'll you do if we survive this one?'

Hargon smiled. 'I think I'll show my paintings to more people. I've always been scared. What if they don't like my art? Or what if they make rude comments?'

Bar Witch sat on the cart. 'You can't please everyone. Trust me.'

'Yeah.' Hargon joined her.

'When the old tavern used to be packed we had all sorts and I don't think I ever had an entire room be completely happy. There's always one, but that's normal. I've had ale thrown at me, an empty cup whack my head. Once, I did a dance and someone rushed the stage and swung his sword at my legs.'

Hargon's eyes widened and Bar Witch laughed.

'Thanks for being the calm one,' Bar Witch said.

'Thanks for being the strong one,' Hargon replied.

Hargon surprised her. She had dreaded being stuck in this situation with him, but now she couldn't think of anyone better to suffer this responsibility with.

She spotted Peezant flying towards the castle. 'Might be news. Let's get back,' she said.

SHARED VISION

Sabrinia entered a wide corridor. Steel panels had fallen away from the cavity-ridden, rocky walls.

Opposite her, fallen rocks blocked a steel door.

The grunting grew.

Frong unsheathed his spear and faced the stairs. 'We'll hold them off. Oaf, you take the door.' Frong chucked a throwing axe into a Gygus' neck, knocking it down and creating a pile-up. 'That'll give us some time.'

Sabrinia fired arrows into the darkness of the staircase while Arazod waited, clutching a loose rock.

'Oaf, how's it going?' Sabrinia shouted.

A large rock flew past them and bashed a Gygus. 'All done,' Oaf said.

They turned to join him but a fleshy tongue grabbed Frong's face and dragged him into a hole in the wall.

'Frong!' Sabrinia's neck tensed and she turned to the others. She wanted to dive into the hole to find Frong but a swarm of Gygus filled the corridor. 'Run!'

Arazod grabbed Frong's spear and they sprinted through the steel door.

They passed more chambers containing hooks and blood-stained steel tables.

'Those pests don't stop running,' Arazod complained.

Sabrinia turned and fired more arrows. In the corner of her eye the tongue shot out towards her.

Oaf pushed her to the floor. 'Sorry.' He extended his hand.

'It's appreciated.' She grabbed his hand and stood.

'Probably best not to stop,' Oaf said and smiled.

The tongue wrapped around his neck.

'Oaf!' Sabrinia reached for Oaf's hand, but he was gone.

'Save my boy!' Oaf screamed and vanished into a cavity.

Sabrinia chased him and climbed into the hole, but Arazod grabbed her leg and pulled her out.

'Get off me!' She kicked.

'You don't go running into the mouth of a beast,' Arazod said.

'We need to save him and Frong!' She pushed Arazod away.

He raised his claws. 'We need to get the gauntlet, then we stand more of a chance of saving them.'

He had a point. If Oaf and Frong were still alive.

The Gygus closed in, but the tongue wrapped around three of them at once, scaring other Gygus away.

Sabrinia took a breath. 'Let's get the damn thing and burn that stupid tongue!' She'd cook it and feed it to Peezant.

They passed more torture chambers.

'I think you should reconsider keeping the gauntlet. You'd be able to handle that power,' Arazod said.

'Right now I just want my friends back.'

They entered a steel honeycomb with a large pit in the middle.

Frong, Oaf and some Gygus lay slumped against the far wall, covered in webbing. Fleshy tongues poked out of the wall and sucked on their heads.

Sabrinia worried the tongues would devour her friends like the skeletal Man-Hawk in webbing next to them.

Sabrinia approached and stabbed an arrow into the tongues attached to her friends, forcing them back into the wall.

Smashed skeletons occupied a chamber. One had a crown hanging off its skull. There it was on her arm – the gauntlet.

Sabrinia approached the chamber.

A Gygus landed in her path and swiped its claws at her.

She dodged and punched it, then jammed an arrow in its eye.

The creature shrieked and fell into the pit.

'Duck!' Arazod yelled from across the pit.

The tongue brushed Sabrinia's head.

'Look.' Arazod pointed to the holes. A faint glow appeared in the holes, perhaps the creature's eyes.

'Let's test it.' Sabrinia faced the glowing spot. The tongue shot out and she dodged. She shot an arrow at the next glow she saw and the beast screeched.

'Behind you!' Arazod yelled.

The tongue whacked her and knocked her over the rocky ledge. She dangled over the pit.

Arazod grabbed her wrists.

The glow appeared in a hole behind him.

'It's coming,' she said.

Arazod swung her onto the ledge and rolled out of the way.

The tongue lashed and retracted.

'You get the gauntlet. I'll distract it,' Arazod said.

Sabrinia ran for the gauntlet.

Arazod dodged tongue attacks.

Sabrinia pulled the gauntlet off Seliria's hand. She put it on and wasn't sure what to do. She ran her hand along the yellow markings but nothing happened.

One of the skeletons by Seliria held a bow and an arrow more impressive than she'd ever seen. She took the bow, much lighter than her own. She lifted the arrow, covered in markings and with three holes in the middle of the shaft.

'Hurry!' Arazod backed into a chamber with nowhere to go.

The gauntlet had a needle on the inside and sat above Sabrinia's vein.

Sabrinia pressed it into her skin and a crystal on the gauntlet glowed green. Warmth filled her veins. She felt at one with fire. She willed her hand to be consumed by flame and it was. She stepped out of the chamber and sent flames shooting into the holes.

'Sabrinia, wait for my signal,' Arazod said.

He stood in the doorway of the chamber and held Frong's spear. The tongue fired at him but he sidestepped. He jammed the spear through the fleshy rope. The beast tried to retract its tongue but the spear held it in the doorway.

'Now, Sabrinia!'

She ran at the tongue and leapt, wrapping her arms and legs around it. She set herself on fire. All around her, flames licked; it was eerily calming.

Shrieking echoed through the room until the tongue flopped to the floor and the noise stopped.

Sabrinia lay on the ground catching her breath. The tongue bled and blistered.

Arazod offered Sabrinia his arm. She gave him an appreciative half smile. 'Let's free the others.'

They ran over to Frong and Oaf and she pulled at the webbing on Frong's face. It was tough.

'We need a knife, or maybe your claws will work.'

He didn't respond.

'Arazod?' She turned around and a spear whacked her across the head.

CHANGE THE WORLD

$\mathcal{K}$arl struggled to focus.

Marlens stroked watery lotion into his hand but he groaned, worried the skin would come off his flesh if she rubbed too hard.

'Hold on, Karl.' Marlens sprang to her feet, grabbed a jar and left the room.

'What's going on? Don't leave me,' he strained, trying to sit up on the steel.

She had left him before and thrown some exploding jars.

'Phew,' she said. 'I thought it was more of those weird creatures.'

She must have been speaking to the others. Karl used his shield to force himself to his feet. Had they succeeded?

'Where are the others?' Marlens asked.

'Please move,' Arazod said. 'I don't want to hurt you.'

'What have you done?' Marlens asked.

Karl stumbled out of the room.

Flames engulfed Arazod's body and he threw a fireball at Marlens. Karl knocked her out of the way and shielded himself from the fire. The heat stung him.

'Don't get in my way!' Arazod said.

Karl struggled to his feet and stumbled over to Marlens. 'Marlens...' He turned her over. She was barely conscious and her head bled.

'Go,' she slurred. 'Stop him.'

Karl dragged his legs and followed Arazod to the top of a cliff, illuminated by the night sun.

Arazod, no longer on fire, stood with his back to Karl.

Ryza and two Man-Hawks hovered above him. She held the blade that had ended Sags' life, and her Man-Hawks waved flaming branches.

Karl hid behind a rock.

'Well done, Little Arazod,' Ryza said. 'I'm glad I didn't chop your head off.'

Flames surrounded Arazod's body and he sent a ball of fire towards Ryza.

She pulled one of her soldiers in the way and shielded her face with a wing. The soldier shrieked, blackened and crumbled; his life reduced to ash, blown away in the wind.

'What are you doing, Ryza?' the other Man-Hawk said.

Arazod sent more fire towards her, but she sacrificed her second soldier and then flew far from Arazod.

'Die!' Arazod yelled, firing fireball after fireball, but she was out of his range.

'Are you done?' Ryza asked.

'I'll be done when you're dead!' he said.

'And when you kill me, how do you plan to leave this island?' Ryza pointed to the ship, a flaming coffin.

Arazod's eyes widened. 'No!' He fired at Ryza. 'No, no, no!' He fired and fired. His feathers stood on end. He screamed into the sky, then sat.

'You've made your point, Little Arazod, but I'll always be a step ahead of you, because I know what goes on in your tiny mind.' Ryza landed and walked towards him.

'Stop!' He aimed his hand towards her.

Karl hoped he'd torch her, then himself.

Ryza raised her arms and placed her sword on the cliff. 'Join me, brother. I will see to it you finally have the love you've always wanted.'

Karl stepped out from behind the rock. 'Don't do it, Arazod. Burn her! We'll find a way back.'

Arazod turned to Karl and looked apologetic. 'The problem with good people, Karl, is that you don't understand power.' He touched the gauntlet. 'You would destroy something so—' he wheezed. 'Magical. You want to keep the world the same, but I want to change it.'

Karl stepped towards him, knowing he could be turned to ash in an instant. 'We don't want to keep the world the same; we want to protect it.'

Arazod's shoulders hung.

'Ignore him, brother,' Ryza said. 'I will make you my second in command.'

'She's just using you, Arazod. You know that,' Karl said.

Arazod shook his head at Karl. 'Isn't that all anyone ever does? Uses?' He gasped. 'I want to be on the winning team, Karl. I want to be—' He wheezed. 'Part of the change, instead of being crushed by it.'

He turned to his sister and nodded. 'Second in command?'

'Arazod…' Karl said. How could he do this?

Ryza nodded. 'Let's get you home.' She picked up her sword. 'But first.' She pointed the Grave Blade at Karl and lunged at him. He blocked with his shield but fell back, too weak to fight, and his hand stung. She stared down at him.

'Stop,' Arazod told her. 'Killing him is too kind, Ryza.' He faced Karl. 'There's no way off the island—' he wheezed. 'Let them starve to death or be eaten by creatures.'

Ryza chuckled. 'You're quite good at being evil.'

'If there's one thing Father taught me, it was how to be horrible.'

Ryza lifted Arazod under his arms and they flew away.

Karl wished he'd driven his sword through Arazod's spine.

THE WRECKAGE OF FAILURE

arl came up for air with bits of the ship in his hands.

'Sags!' Frong dived into the dark wreckage again. Wood burned on top of the sea; no matter how many times Frong and Karl dived, Karl knew it was pointless. He wanted to stop Frong, but how could he? All Frong had was the hope that he might find his dead lover only partially charred.

Frong surfaced and Sabrinia held his shoulders. 'You need to rest, Frong.'

'I need to find Sags. That's what I need to do.' He dived back in.

Sabrinia looked at Karl. 'You're not helping.'

'That's exactly what I am doing.' Karl dived. The water soothed his burnt hand. He found nothing so returned.

'How are we supposed to get back?' Oaf sculpted rocks into planks, trying to make a boat.

Even if he made something big enough, without sails they'd be rowing for the rest of their lives.

'If I ever see Arazod again I'll snap his neck.' Oaf stopped pounding the rocks and stared out at the empty ocean. 'What about Questions and Quizmal?'

'Let's go back inside Seliria's lair. Maybe there's something that can help us,' Marlens suggested.

Anger rose in Karl's body. If he'd killed Arazod when he had the chance, none of this would've happened. He hated them for trusting Arazod and for making Karl think he could.

They would likely die here. There would be no resurrection, no saving Oaf's son, no saving Flowfornians, and no redemption. The world would fall and those unfortunate enough to be kept alive would live with Man-Hawk screeches piercing their ears until they died.

Karl walked away, up the mountain.

'Where are you going?' Sabrinia asked.

'Away.' Karl walked to the cliff where Arazod had condemned him to death and sat on the edge.

'You okay?' Sabrinia sat next to him.

'What's the point in any of it?' Karl asked. 'When I just existed and ate honey-covered beans, ignorant to everything, life was fine. Boring but fine. Now, every day, even in the last few years of peace, I worry that we'll be attacked. Is that what life is? Constantly waiting for the next evil to fight until eventually one just kills me? That's not a life.' He hated himself for thinking it. 'Sorry, I know it's selfish.'

Sabrinia put her hand on his good one. 'It's not. Living without struggling against the world should be the minimum, but the world isn't like that. And you were never good at being a bean-eating stray. There was a long list of people who wanted to hurt you.'

They chuckled.

'True. Proster for one.' Karl smiled.

Sabrinia rested her head on his shoulder. 'It's not about us, Karl. It never has been. It's about preparing the world for others. It might feel like we're fighting a never-ending tide of evil, and that when one wave settles another larger one forms on the horizon, but we have to believe that each victory gives the future a chance. If we let ourselves get washed away without fighting back, the future gets washed away too.'

'But isn't the future just the same cycle but with different people?'

'We have to believe it won't be, that evil is an illness that can be cured and one day the world will be the one we hope for. Otherwise what's the point in any of it?'

Karl took a breath and squeezed her hand. She was right. 'I just want it to be a bit easier.'

She turned to him and they kissed. He would fight for their future.

'Karl! Sabrinia!' Marlens yelled and ran up to them. 'Could use a hand or two.'

They returned to the shore. Oaf stood in front of Frong, waist deep in the sea.

'Just eat me! I don't care!' Frong waved his spear at a mass of Gygus behind a ten-foot high wall of fire Marlens created.

'He doesn't mean it,' Oaf said to the Gygus, raising a hand. 'Go and eat some rocks or something instead. We're not so tasty.'

'Come on!' Frong stepped towards the Gygus, but Oaf held him back.

Frong hit Oaf's arms. 'Let me die! I'll take a handful of them with me.'

Karl and the others stood in front of them. 'If we're going to die here, Frong, it'll be from starvation and no hope of leaving the island, not from getting eaten by these weird yet terrifying things.' Karl raised his shield, gripping it as well as he could.

'How long does that fire last, Marlens?' Oaf asked.

'Not long enough,' she replied.

The wall of fire lowered to Karl's height.

'Frong,' Sabrinia said. 'Some advice would be handy right about now.'

Oaf turned Frong to face him. 'Sags would want you to go on, Frong… And… Well… I need to see my wife and son.' He welled up.

Frong's breathing slowed and he nodded to Oaf. 'Higher ground.'

Karl ran towards the edge of a cliff and the rest followed.

The fire vanished.

'Prepare your weapons, stay in a bunch, and aim to knock them off the cliff.' Frong drew his spear.

The Gygus' growls chilled Karl's body. He held his shield up and peered at the path. 'I don't suppose you have a few more of those flaming bottles, Marlens?'

'Nope.'

The growls neared and the beasts charged up the path. A blur of arms, claws, and bodies bumped against Karl's shield.

'Hold!' Frong said.

Karl's feet shuffled back and his ruined hand stung.

The Gygus pounded at them and Karl's right foot stroked the cliff edge.

'I can't keep this up!' Sabrinia jabbed an arrow into the neck of a Gygus.

'We have to attack!' Karl broke out of the group and charged.

'No, Karl!' Frong cried out.

Karl whacked his shield into a Gygus, then another, but a claw scratched his ribs and neck and he fell to the floor. Teeth sunk into his leg and he stared at the night sky, worried it would be the last thing he saw.

Yellow-finned sharks leapt over him and their tentacles whipped the Gygus.

Three of the blue creatures repelled the Gygus. One of them whistled and a yellow-finned shark leapt over Karl. Its tentacles grabbed him and whipped him into the air, and then he fell towards the sea.

LETTING GO

'Thanks,' Karl told the blue, muscular being, standing on her yellow-finned shark in the shallows. The rest of her people sat on their beasts. Karl worried they might still decide to eat them. His leg stung from the bite and blood dotted his shirt from the scratches.

'Thank you,' the blue creature said in a low voice. 'For saving us from the Klongryth.'

'Is that the giant horrible thing that attacked us?'

The blue creature nodded. 'One of Octorion's pets. She took humans as husbands, but her insane jealousy consumed her and she would experiment on her lovers as punishment, binding them to beasts and creating hybrids. Then when she got fed up she would cast her beasts into the sea – our sea.'

Karl rubbed his neck. 'Sorry.'

'We lost thousands of Shalas over time, but the Klongryth was the worst beast. Thirty sunsets we fought it and it still wouldn't die, so we chained it to the depths. We're meant to stop people entering that particular part of the sea, but we got lazy. It had been thousands of sunsets since anyone came along.'

Karl sat on the shore. 'Well, we're not going anywhere now, so no danger of us waking it again.'

'We will return you to your home,' she said.

Karl heart lightened. Was that even possible?

Sabrinia approached. 'Can you help us fight a different kind of beast?'

'We won't last long out of the sea. So unless the battle is near an ocean, we're of little use to you.'

Karl hoped the home he returned to was still there, and that Oaf's boy was still alive.

The Shala's shark swam up to Karl. He backed off.

'It's fine. Trust her,' the Shala said.

The shark attached a tentacle to Karl's leg wound and healed it. Karl thought he'd better stroke its head as thanks. Another tentacle met Karl's burned hand and a chill shot through it. His fingers cramped and his wrist stung, but then his hand tingled and it was healed. Were these things magical? Karl's hand felt stronger than it did before he had set it alight.

Another Shala, smaller than the leader, emerged from the depths and whispered to her. The leader nodded. The Shala approached Frong and offered him a skeletal hand.

Frong stared at it. 'Sags?'

The Shala handed it over. 'I'm sorry. It's all I could recover.'

Frong held it and wept.

'Hey,' Karl said. 'We can still do this. If we get the soul back we can bring him back. We'll use that lizard hair thing and restore his body, then we resurrect him. There's still hope, Frong!'

Frong touched Karl's arm and shook his head. 'Your optimism is appreciated, Karl, but it's over. It was over the moment he drew his last breath. He's gone but I can make sure I never forget him.'

'Like my mum.' Karl welled up. Letting go didn't mean letting go; it meant trying to move forwards and carrying the memories.

Frong nodded. 'I'm happy to have a part of him. Even if it is quite haunting.' He stared at the hand. 'You know, in some cultures, people keep the skeletons of their dead in a room where they place them in living positions, so they're still there.' He took a breath and used Sags' hand to scratch his beard. 'At least he can still do nice things for me.'

Karl smiled.

Sabrinia addressed them. 'Our mission is clear. We kill Ryza and save Oaf's boy. We also need to recover the Soul of Illuminus so we can gain control of Death. Let's save the world so we can enjoy the memories we have of our loved ones.'

Frong gazed at Sags' hand, illuminated by the night sun. 'Thank you, Sags. Life can be a book of beautiful adventures. You taught me how to read it.'

SIBLING PRISONER

$\mathcal{A}$razod stared at the horizon, willing land to appear.

'This sea never ends.' Ryza stopped and hovered, holding Arazod above the water.

'It can't be much further. You don't want to keep Death waiting,' Arazod said. He considered setting her ablaze, but he'd be stranded at sea. He could do it for the good of the world, but he wouldn't get to see it. He wouldn't benefit.

'You're right.' Ryza continued flying.

Land formed in the distance. Arazod would have his moment and enjoy the aftermath. He'd burn her in front of the others and they'd swear allegiance to him.

Ryza released Arazod's arms.

'Ryza!' Arazod crashed into the cold ocean. His heart raced and he thrashed his arms. 'Ryza! Get me out! It's freezing.'

She smirked in that way. The way that made him feel pathetic. 'Give me the gauntlet, Little Arazod.'

'Yes! Once we get to the tower.' Arazod kicked his legs to stay afloat.

Ryza chuckled. 'You have a choice. You give me the gauntlet

now and we go. Or you stay here. You could die by drowning or die when a sea creature is in the mood for a snack.'

Arazod stared at her. He couldn't be at her mercy again. He winced at the sight of her blade, a reminder of his wings being hacked off.

'You see, Little Arazod,' she said. 'Never forget. I'll always be smarter than you.'

She controlled his life again.

A SHORT REUNION

Questions hid behind the rubble of a collapsed staircase on an upper floor of the broken Lookout Tower.

Her hands trembled. Although Peezant told her to wait, she poked her head out from behind the rubble.

Through a window, four Man-Hawks carried an empty cage and landed in the debris-covered courtyard.

Peezant returned and perched on Questions' shoulder. 'He's up there.' He pointed his beak up another floor she'd have to climb.

'Are you sure?' she asked, relieved her boy was alive.

'No,' Peezant said. 'It must have been someone else's half Oaf, half Inquiso son. There are so many of those around.'

'Really?' she asked.

Peezant stared at her. 'Just follow me,' he squawked and flew up. He waved her up with his wing.

She placed her foot on a rock, pushed herself onto a broken doorframe and climbed. The wind blew where walls used to be. She ran along the corridor. Her heart pounded, excited and terrified to see her boy.

Peezant flapped his wings and turned back. He flew in front of her face.

'What are you doing?' She waved him away.

'Shush. Hide in here.' He flew into a room without a wall.

'Why?' Questions followed and ducked behind a cupboard.

Was something bad happening? Were those Quizmal's cries?

'Stupid little runt,' a Man-Hawk shouted.

Was that a claw slicing flesh?

'You have to wait, Questions,' Peezant said.

Were they beating her boy?

What would her father do? Would he wait? Did he tell her that protecting people sometimes meant waiting?

Tears filled her eyes. Was that another slash?

The Man-Hawk flew out of the room and back to the courtyard.

Peezant flew to the room and waved Questions over.

She ran to him and her heart swelled. She kneeled and held Quizmal. The emptiness disappeared and for a moment she forgot about the danger that hung over them. 'Do I love you?'

'Ma!' Quizmal squeezed her.

She held his face and stared at his scratched cheeks. She kissed the marks.

'Who are you?' A Man-Hawk stood in the doorway, sword drawn.

'Am I his ma?' Questions stood and clenched her dagger.

'I don't know. Are you?' the Man-Hawk asked.

Peezant perched on her shoulder.

'Am I?' she answered.

The Man-Hawk huffed. 'Why are you being confusing?'

Peezant shook his feathers. 'She can only speak in questions. A curse, or a disability, or something. Not really sure, to be honest. She could even just be doing it for effect or as part of a long joke.'

Was that Quizmal's blood on the Man-Hawk's claws? Questions' blood boiled.

'Do you have any last words? Or last questions?' The Man-Hawk asked.

'Will you let us leave?' she asked.

'That's a rubbish last question. Of course not.' He drew his sword back.

Questions held Quizmal and closed her eyes.

Did something hit her feet?

She opened her eyes and the Man-Hawk lay face down.

Hargon and Bar Witch stood in the doorway and Questions' body shook.

Bar Witch wiped the bloody sword on her tunic.

'Hello there,' Hargon smiled.

'Did you save us?' Questions pressed her hands to her mouth.

'Yep.' Bar Witch nodded and sheathed the sword. She dragged the Man-Hawk's body into the cupboard.

'Let's get you out of here,' Hargon said.

They snuck through the corridor and waited at the entrance to the Lookout Tower. They waited a while, then a while longer.

Why weren't the Man-Hawks moving?

'I wonder how Alf is doing,' Hargon said.

'Alf? Is that what you're calling the baby?' Bar Witch asked.

'Yeah, rhymes with Walty, the name of my old dead dog.'

'Does it rhyme with Walty?' Questions asked.

Bar Witch shook her head. 'Don't waste your time, Questions.'

Squawks and shrieks filled the sky.

'They'll be on us soon,' Hargon said.

'What do we do?' Questions asked.

A beaked shadow crept around the corner, and another.

Hargon took a breath. 'I'll fix this.' He edged out of hiding.

'No, Hargon. Wait until it quietens,' Bar Witch said.

'I have to do something, otherwise we're all done.' He shrugged, drew his sword and walked towards the Man-Hawks.

'Hargon!' Bar Witch stepped out but Questions pulled her back.

'Is he doing this for us?' Questions asked.

Bar Witch hung her head.

Questions squeezed Quizmal's hand.

'Hey! Red head. What are you doing?' a Man-Hawk called out.

'Hi. I was walking through the forest and thought I'd come and see this place. It's just like in the stories.'

The shadows vanished from around Questions.

Man-Hawks surrounded Hargon.

'Visitors aren't welcome anymore.' A Man-Hawk drew her sword.

Bar Witch gripped her blade.

'Is the safest place the room we came from?' Questions asked.

Bar Witch nodded, her face sad.

Hargon placed his sword on the pebbles and addressed his captor. 'You know, I think I understand what being a good leader is now.'

'Stop talking,' the Man-Hawk said.

'It's about looking after others ahead of yourself. Thinking about the future.' Hargon looked towards Bar Witch. 'I hope someone looks after Alf.'

'Who's Alf?' a Man-Hawk said.

'A baby I met in a village not far from here. His name made me smile because it rhymes with my old dog's name.'

'What was your dog's name?'

'Walty.'

The Man-Hawk scrunched his beak. 'Those names don't rhyme.'

'Who are you? The god of rhymes? If I want it to be a rhyme, it is,' Hargon said.

'Shut up.' The Man-Hawk pointed his sword towards the cage. 'Get in.'

Hargon stepped into the cage.

Questions and Bar Witch watched from the broken wall of an upper floor. Hargon saw them and smiled at them.

Questions shed a tear and Bar Witch bit her lip.

Questions couldn't believe he was sacrificing himself to help them. They had to succeed.

HOMEWARD

If someone asked Karl what the weirdest thing he could imagine was, he could never have conjured the image of riding a shark with tentacles, navigated by a weird blue creature.

The sun set, a purple blanket over the sea. Hastovia in its purest form. Water, sky and wind. No castles or man-made obstructions. Or death.

Sabrinia showed Frong an arrow. 'I found this in Seliria's palace.'

Frong took the arrow and ran his finger over the markings. 'Rune markings.' He held it out in front of him. 'An energy weapon.'

Karl looked at Sabrinia and shrugged. Here comes a story.

Frong returned the arrow to Sabrinia. 'When the gods didn't want to do their own dirty work, they entrusted special weapons to a group of hunters. Gods and descendants of gods are immortal, so unless they kill each other, the only way to kill them is with these energy weapons.'

'So we have a chance against Death?' Sabrinia said.

Frong shook his head. 'Not so much. He's not exactly going to charge the weapon himself, and I don't know any descendant of the gods. Do you?'

Sabrinia shook her head.

Karl tapped the Shala controlling his shark. 'Are your people linked to the gods in any way?'

The Shala shook her head. 'Only in that we have to keep clearing their mess.'

'Sorry it's not more useful,' Frong said. 'Anyway. I need to rest.' The shark's tentacles wrapped around Frong and he closed his eyes.

Sabrinia put the arrow away and gazed at the sunset. 'Stunning, isn't it? It's strange to think under such beauty there can be so much horror and nonsense.'

Karl nodded. 'It's more magical than any god-made relic. But I'd be able to appreciate it more if I didn't have wet trousers and underwear.'

Sabrinia chuckled. 'Yes. I don't really feel like going into battle wearing just a breastplate.' She shrugged. 'Who knows, maybe it'll provide a distraction that gives us the upper hand.'

Karl smiled and dipped his fingers in the water, letting the sea flow through them. 'Do you think what we're going through is happening somewhere else in the world? Or do you think everywhere else is peaceful?'

Sabrinia looked Karl in the eyes. 'I hope it's peaceful. But even in peace there are other battles. Personal ones.' She broke eye contact. 'I know even with everyone loving him, Father had problems of sadness.'

'I'm sorry,' Karl said.

Sabrinia dipped her hands in the water, then ran her fingers through her hair. 'He lived in fear of tragedy, and it stopped him being able to commit to loving.'

Life was a series of battles, inner and outer. Karl couldn't have hoped for a better group of friends to go through the battles with. His mind drifted to thoughts of the coming conflict. How would they defeat Ryza? She was faster, stronger, more willing to kill. Add to that a flaming gauntlet and Death and Karl stood no chance. He recalled their brief battle. Every strike was blocked before it was even close.

Sabrinia's shark swam next to Karl's.

Sabrinia grabbed Karl's hand. 'I'm sorry you didn't get more time with your mother, Karl.'

He exhaled. 'I wish I could've just asked her a few more questions. They're always knocking around in my mind.'

Sabrinia stroked the back of her shark. 'You'll always have more questions, Karl. And we never get enough time with those we love. You had less time than is fair, but in that brief moment, I saw more love than most experience in a lifetime.'

Tears filled Karl's eyes. He stared at Sabrinia's gentle but tired face. She made his life worth living. He finally understood what Illuminus meant when she screamed, 'Life is death.' For the rest of the journey, all Karl could do was hope that Sabrinia would forgive him for what he planned to do…

PLANNING PROBLEMS

'Are you mad?' Frong grabbed Karl's arm.

'Quiet.' Karl didn't want Sabrinia to hear. He approached the group's clothes, drying over a fire.

Sabrinia fired arrows at trees across the stream.

'There'll be a better way, Karl.' Frong pulled his beard over his naked lower half.

'Yeah, this is dumb,' Oaf said.

Marlens nodded and adjusted her potion belt to cover her naked body.

'It's the only way we have a chance.' Karl sat on a tree stump and placed his shield over his genitals. 'When I fought Ryza, she was too fast and too strong. Easily the strongest creature or person I've ever fought.'

Oaf raised a finger. 'You've only had about six fights. I'll take her.'

Karl wished he could accept Oaf's offer. 'Killing isn't in you, Oaf. That's where she has the advantage. Any hesitation and it's death to us.'

'For Quizmal and Questions, I'll kill everything. And if I see Arazod I'll crush his skull,' Oaf said.

Karl didn't doubt that. 'You, Marlens and Sabrinia need to find Questions and Quizmal first. Us two will take Ryza. Hopefully Hargon, Bar Witch, and whoever else they've found can help.'

Marlens touched her wet clothes. 'What if your plan don't work, Karl? You'll be dead for nothin'.'

Karl shrugged. 'If I don't try, we'll all be dead for nothing.'

Frong dug his upper teeth into his beard. 'Please, Karl...'

'Sags taught me a valuable lesson,' Karl said. 'And it was how to find an opening. I'll create it, then you chop her head off and get the orb. Please don't tell Sabrinia.'

They stood in silence, made uncomfortable by their semi-nudity. One way or another, they were one sunset away from the end.

HARGON

*H*argon leaned his head against the cage. Scattered bodies dotted the snow.

It made no sense. It was warm, but that circle – it was as if someone had taken the tower from the coldest part of Hastovia and moved it, bringing the weather with it.

He'd seen a magic relic at work, but this was weird. He'd love to paint it. A tower with a snowy tower around it. He'd hang it in his room next to the painting of Arazod in the dungeon.

First, he had to survive.

A group of Flowfornians held torches and Man-Hawks forced them into the snow. Two steps and they froze, fell, and never rose again.

The Man-Hawks covered a woman in steel armour and threw a sheet over her. They set her on fire and pushed her towards the tower. Two steps and she fell, her screams disappearing under the snow.

One push of Hargon's cage and he and twenty Flowfornians would roll towards the same end.

Was this it? He imagined dying of old age, peacefully. He hoped Alf would get a chance to live in more peaceful times.

Man-Hawks draped cloaks over the cage.

'It's fine, we're warm enough already,' Hargon said.

A Man-Hawk poked its sword through the bars. 'Shut up!'

'Rude,' Hargon replied.

Another Man-Hawk poured oil over the cloaks while another lit a torch. Hargon's fellow prisoners huddled into the centre of the cage.

Hargon closed his eyes. He should've taken his art to villages and kingdoms. Maybe he would've made it as a touring artist. Maybe they'd discover his talent in death. If the realm of the dead was real at least he could enjoy success from afar.

'Good luck, Questions and Bar Witch. It's been a pleasure.' It was like there was a spike in his stomach. He closed his eyes, but wild screeching interrupted. He pushed his way to the back of the cage and peered through a gap in the cloaks.

Arazod landed with a Man-Hawk wearing a gauntlet, no doubt Ryza.

The Man-Hawks drew their weapons and surrounded Arazod.

Ryza smirked.

'You said!' Arazod yelled. 'You said they would accept me!'

Ryza chuckled. 'Rest your weapons,' she commanded.

The Man-Hawks relaxed their stances.

Ryza pointed at Arazod. 'Little Arazod is a hero. He found the gauntlet.'

The arrogance Hargon associated with Arazod was gone.

Ryza's body ignited. Why wasn't she screaming?

'That's amazing,' Arnul said.

'It feels amazing too,' she said. 'When the spike inside the gauntlet pierced my skin, my veins felt at one with the heat. I am fire.' She chuckled.

'What do you want me to do with these?' Arnul pointed to the cage.

Ryza shrugged. 'We no longer need to test the magic. I have my way in.'

Hargon's heart lightened, pleased to be free of a frosty death.

'But push them in anyway. Saves us carrying them back.' Ryza disappeared into the frost.

'Wait! No!' Hargon yelled.

The cage rolled.

'Please!' He shook the bars, hoping he could stop it or make it fall.

A cold energy surrounded his body and gripped his bones, lungs and heart.

He stopped breathing.

A DEADLY RESURRECTION

*R*yza flew up through the dark tower and checked every room. She didn't care about the statues, the books, the treasure chests, the markings on the walls or what they meant. She only wanted to see her prize, her new ally.

She reached the highest chamber of the tower. Death was twice her size and frozen to the ceiling. His lifeless face and hollow dark eyes faced the tiled floor. Rune markings covered the wall and a line of blue stones circled a yellow crystal beneath him.

Ryza approached the circle of stones.

The far wall moved and the ice formed into a ghoul. It floated towards Ryza. Its piercing blue eyes shot open and its mouth released a blast of blue flame.

Ryza shot fire. It blasted through the blue and vanquished the ghoul.

'So easy.' She laughed and blasted the blue stones away. She placed her claws on the yellow crystal and heated it until it shattered.

The ice melted away, as did the barrier to her dominating Hastovia.

Ryza waited for Death to fall, but he floated onto his feet and the smoky black in his hollow eyes fixed on her. He had no weapon, but nails like sharp teeth. A terrifying energy poured off him. Ryza realised she was insignificant in comparison to this god.

'Thank you for freeing me,' Death said.

Ryza shook her head. 'You're mistaken, Death. You are not free.'

'You are foolish.' Death raised a hand to strike.

'Uh uh.' Ryza held out the Soul of Illuminus and set her hand ablaze.

'Stop!' Death lowered his hand. 'Do not harm her.'

Ryza smirked. The power of love. The strongest weakness. 'On your knees,' she commanded.

Death lowered to his knees.

Ryza had true power, true significance. 'I own you.'

A NEW POWER

*A*razod faced the Great Dragon's cave. That's what he'd become – bait. He turned to Ryza at the end of the path. 'We don't need to—' he wheezed and struggled.

'Out with it!' Arnul said and the Man-Hawks laughed.

'We don't need to do this,' Arazod said.

'It's fine, Little Arazod.' Ryza flew above him. 'Dragon! We have something for you.'

Arazod stared into the darkness.

The low growl carried the stench of boar-hippo, a reminder of two miserable years.

'Pidgy!' the Great Dragon roared. 'You had me worried.' Its amber eyes pierced the black. 'Get back in here and make my teeth squeaky-clean. The grot has built up for far too long.' The Great Dragon blinked. 'More pigeons. This is nice.'

Arazod hoped the Great Dragon would burn them all.

Ryza held the orb and turned to Death. 'Kill it.'

'Dragons are sacred,' Death said.

'And a nuisance.' Ryza's hand flamed. 'Get on with it.'

Death turned to the dragon. 'Know that I do not want this.' He hovered towards the dragon and stood next to Arazod.

Arazod ran back to Ryza.

'If that's the way it is...' The Great Dragon roared, flew up and engulfed Death in fire. When the smoke cleared, Death was gone and the dragon landed.

Was that it?

The dragon smiled. 'Silly pigeons. Now it's your turn.' His eyes glowed red and the pulsing flame created cracks in his neck. He opened his mouth, but Death appeared next to the dragon's throat and sliced it open with a swipe of the hand.

Arazod shuddered.

The dragon shrieked and its face slammed against the mountain path.

Death placed his hand on the dragon's head and its eyes dulled and crumbled. 'I'm sorry.' Death hung his head.

Dragon blood flowed over the side of the mountain and towards Arazod. It was too swift. Too simple.

'Back here.' Ryza pointed to her side.

Death joined her.

'Well done,' Ryza said to him. 'All of you, chop the dragon up and take a piece of it to any castle and city you can find. Make leaders an offer. Serve our army, or live in the knowledge that their final day is coming.' Ryza placed a claw on Arazod's shoulder. 'And you should all thank Little Arazod. He made this all possible, and is now my second in command.'

The Man-Hawks dropped to their knees and chanted.

'General Arazod! General Arazod!'

This was it, the moment he'd always wished for. They cheered him and smiled at him, but it was empty.

'Now, Death. I'd like to speak to my father,' Ryza said.

Arazod's neck feathers stood on end.

A blue aura surrounded Death.

'Are you planning on resurrecting him?' Arazod wished he'd destroyed their father's body when he killed him, but he wanted to visit it from time to time to remind himself of his victory. To him, Sarzo's body was a trophy.

'Don't worry your mind, Little General Arazod,' Ryza replied.

Arnul smirked. 'Just let Ryza take care of things and enjoy being part of history.'

Arazod couldn't let her keep this power. She would have to sleep soon, and that's when Death could kill her. And if she gave Arnul the orb to guard, Arazod would kill him and take Death for himself. Ryza might have always been a step ahead, but Arnul was an idiot.

Grey smoke flooded from Death's eyes and covered the blue. A cough carried on the smoke. 'Ryza! You're alive!' Sarzo's voice was like a dagger to the stomach.

'And you! Ryza, resurrect me so I can rip him apart,' Sarzo said.

'I will soon, Father,' Ryza replied.

'Supreme Man-Hawk Sarzo,' he corrected.

'Sorry. Supreme Man-Hawk Sarzo,' Ryza said with a hint of irritation.

Arnul dropped to a knee.

'Where are you?' Ryza asked.

'I don't know. But it's miserable, and swords fly independently of a master, keeping me from exploring parts of this rocky dump. I've had to align myself with an idiot to survive.'

Ryza took a scroll from inside her armour and unrolled it. 'I need you to tell me where the Stone of Eternity is.'

'No,' Sarzo said. 'That power is for me.'

'Good luck using it where you are,' Ryza said. 'I guess we won't be resurrecting you.'

'Ryza!' his voice shook them.

'Tell me where it is,' she commanded. 'You want resurrection, you tell me.'

'Very well,' his defeated voice said. 'But when you bring me back, I demand time alone with my son.'

Ryza looked at Arazod and her beak curled into a smirk.

Arazod, Ryza and Arnul flew over a forest on an island northwest of Flowfornia.

'This is it,' Ryza said.

They landed inside a circle of giant trees.

Arazod wasn't sure what was going on, but an eerie warmth gripped him.

'These trees are meant to have been destroyed,' Death said.

Ryza leaned on one. 'I'm glad they weren't. Now, the ritual.' She wrapped her hands around the orb. 'You two out,' she told Arnul and Arazod.

They both left the circle of trees.

'You see. Father wasn't after this orb for the purpose of resurrecting anyone or just to command Death. He wanted to use Death to become immortal.'

Every time she opened her mouth, things got worse. Arazod imagined his future, being called Little General Arazod constantly. General by name, outcast in life.

'Death, make me immortal.'

Black tears rolled out of Death's eye sockets. He touched one of the trees. A gash formed in the bark and a green liquid poured onto the soil and surrounded Ryza.

Lines of orange light burst out of the other trees and shone on Ryza.

The green liquid encased her in stone. Hopefully she'd suffocate.

The stone cracked and broke.

No such luck.

Ryza grinned at Death. 'Now I don't need to rest ever again, so there's no chance of you killing me in my sleep.'

Death stared at the soil.

Ryza handed the Grave Blade to Arnul. 'Swing at me.'

Arnul hesitated.

'Just do it,' Ryza ordered.

Arazod hoped her confidence was misplaced and that the blade would chop through her.

Arnul swung. The blade stuck in Ryza's ribs. She laughed and pulled it out. Her wound sealed.

Arazod's body numbed.

'The world is ours,' Ryza declared.

'Are we going to resurrect Supreme Man-Hawk Sarzo now?' Arnul asked.

Ryza smirked. 'He had his chance in this world and he let Little General Arazod better him. My father is where he belongs.'

'But he is our master,' Arnul said.

'Was.' Ryza corrected and stared at Arnul. 'We need to move forwards and discard our failed past.'

Arnul nodded and kneeled. 'Yes, my master.'

Arazod dug his claws into his palms to stop the shaking. He kneeled and stared at the grass. He would never get the better of his sister.

FACING DEATH

Karl pressed his back against Flowforn's wall. His home. A home full of unwanted guests screeching in the night.

'What is that thing?' Marlens pointed to the sky.

A flying cart the size of five.

Three Man-Hawks carried each corner. Chanting and grunting filled the air.

Frong shook his head. 'Seems like the numbers have tipped even more heavily in their favour.'

Karl turned to Oaf. 'The alleys are just over this wall. It'll be easier to sneak through.'

'Okay. Shall we have a look?' Oaf said.

Karl nodded and Oaf lifted him. Karl grabbed the top of the wall and peered over it. Empty. 'Perfect.' He glanced at the destroyed King's Tower and the broken bridge. Parts of the Lookout Tower were missing and he spotted a Man-Hawk pacing along one of the exposed corridors. Karl dropped back down. 'There's a Man-Hawk on an upper floor of the Lookout Tower. I'd say that's where we're likely to find Quizmal and Questions.'

Marlens switched a purple jar with a yellow one on her belt. 'Right. So me and Oaf, we'll look for Questions and Quizmal. Sabrinia, you join us, then get as high as you can to get a good strategic place for shooting them arrows. And you two.' She nodded at Karl and Frong. 'You try to get that orb so we can get control of Death and turn the tide. Got it?'

'Got it,' Sabrinia said. Karl nodded.

Marlens poured the yellow mixture onto the soil. It ate through the dirt, creating a pit. 'Good old octo-eagle stomach acid.' Marlens jumped into the pit and stabbed at the soil beneath the stone wall.

'Oaf,' Karl said. 'If we get through this, do me a favour and put a cage around the pool of tortured souls. That way when you revive another you can put them through a long process of questioning before unleashing a lunatic on the world.' Karl patted his arm.

Oaf jumped into the pit. 'Don't you worry.' He grabbed handfuls of soil and threw them out of the pit. 'I'm never helping a tortured soul again.'

Marlens stopped digging and stared at him. 'If it weren't for you helpin', I'd still be a tortured soul, Karl would've never been cured of petrification, and Arazod would be rulin' Hastovia.'

Oaf stopped digging. 'Sorry... When I have my family back I'll be less grumpy.'

Marlens hugged him. 'We'll do everything we can.'

Oaf bit his bottom lip. He lifted Marlens out of the pit and scooped a handful of dirt. The wall collapsed into the pit and around Oaf.

Karl turned to Sabrinia. 'Let's fix our home and this world.'

She held his hand and kissed him. 'I love you.'

'I love you too,' he said. 'Whatever happens, you've been the best thing in my life.'

She smiled. 'We've still got a lot to experience together.' She stroked her hair out of her face and addressed them all. 'Thank you for everything. Let's try not to die.'

They entered and split into their groups.

Karl and Frong crept through the alleys. No candles shone in the windows and judging by the metallic smell, the blood-stains on the walls were fresh.

'Are you certain about this, Karl?' Frong asked.

He poked his head around a corner. They were close to the courtyard where they'd get more of a sense of what was going on. 'Of course I'm not.'

Frong chuckled, and Karl did too. It warmed his heart that in dark times they could still find something to laugh about.

'Down here,' a woman's voice ordered.

Karl and Frong hid behind an abandoned market stall.

Two Man-Hawks flew around the corner and perched on a house.

'What do we do now we have all this power?' one asked the other.

'Don't know. It's a bit weird, really. You work so hard to do something, then when you get it life just gets boring.'

'Yeah. I never really thought about what comes next.'

'I guess we sort of, just eat loads until we die fat but relaxed.'

They laughed.

Karl stepped out from behind the market stall and laughed with them. 'Hilarious. You're both so funny.'

They looked at each other and drew their shazaqs, but a throwing axe hit one Man-Hawk in the throat, then the other. They dropped to the floor.

Karl took their swords. 'If we find Flowfornians we can arm them.'

Karl and Frong gazed out of the alley and into the courtyard.

Ryza stood in front of a crowd of Man-Hawks and beings Karl had never seen. There was the orb, on a chain around her neck.

Cyclopes with bald women growing out of their necks stood in front of a pile of Flowfornian corpses.

'Next,' Ryza said.

Arazod dragged a rope-bound Flowfornian woman in front of Ryza and then stood by her.

Karl tensed at the sight of Arazod. If he got the chance he'd slit his throat.

'On your knees,' Ryza told the Flowfornian.

The Flowfornian wept and dropped to her knees. Ryza turned to the crowd. 'Keep as a slave or kill?'

The bloodthirsty mob cheered for the kill. Ryza nodded to Death. Death, shoulders slumped, placed his hand on the woman's head, her eyes dulled and she flopped to the floor.

That's how easy it was. They stood no chance against that power.

'It's too crowded for us to attack,' Frong said. 'But a famous warrior once said, if you can't get to the enemy, bring the enemy to you.'

'How do we do that?' Karl asked.

'I don't know. That was all I knew of that warrior. She died quite young. Apparently she invited a group of enemies into her home and it didn't go so well.'

Karl huffed. 'Brilliant.'

'Who are you?' a deep voice said from behind them.

Karl turned to fairy twins holding horns.

'We're one of the armies, here to swear allegiance to our new queen,' Karl said.

Frong nodded. 'That is indeed correct. We're just waiting for a good moment to present ourselves.'

'And which army are you?' one asked.

'Umm...' Karl looked at Frong.

'We're from just beyond the north sea,' he said.

'Oh, the Lansfor army.' One of the fairies smiled.

'Yes. Yes. That's the one.' Frong smiled at Karl.

'Doesn't exist.' The smile vanished and the fairies blew their horns.

UNWANTED RESPONSIBILITY

*B*ar Witch tired of being in the cupboard with Questions and, more annoyingly, a dead Man-Hawk.

She could barely see through the gap in the doors and the stench of death wouldn't escape fast enough. Over the last sunset it had only worsened.

She'd given most of her seeds to Quizmal to stop him whining and they'd missed two chances to attack a Man-Hawk and escape. They couldn't afford to miss another.

'Right. Next time one of those feathered idiots comes through that door, we pounce,' Bar Witch said.

'Who will pounce first?' Questions asked, staring at Quizmal through the gap in the doors.

Bar Witch wondered why people bothered having kids. They just create panic. 'You go first to throw them off guard. I follow and stick them with the sword.' She gripped the Man-Hawk's shazaq.

'What if there are two of them?' Questions asked.

'Well, then the same plan goes, but you take the one that moves closest to the window, and I take the one closest to the door.' She hoped Questions had no more questions.

'What if they stand next to each other?'

Bar Witch huffed. 'Then I'll take the one furthest, so closest to the opposite wall to here. And you take the one closest. Closest to here.' That was every scenario. 'Now let's keep watch.' She enjoyed the silence.

'What if there are three of them?' Questions asked.

Bar Witch clenched her fists. 'Right. Whatever happens, I'll go first and tell you what to do.'

Muffled shouting neared the door to the room.

'What are they saying?' Questions asked.

'I don't know, because you're talking over them.'

A sword clattered off the stone floor and the door opened. 'Shush.' Bar Witch peered towards the door as much as she could. She crouched and pressed a hand against the back of the cupboard to steady herself, ready to leap out. But she recognised the green beast who hugged Quizmal.

'Quizmal!' Oaf burst into tears.

Questions burst out of the cupboard, revealing Sabrinia and Marlens in the doorway stood over a Man-Hawk with an arrow in his neck.

'Questions!' Oaf pulled her into the hug.

Bar Witch swung her legs out of the cupboard and sat. Tears filled her eyes. Maybe that's why people had kids. The love outweighed the pain.

'You crying, Bar Witch?' Marlens asked and gave her a hug.

'Just relieved I can get out of here,' she said. 'So stuffy.'

Oaf covered Quizmal's eyes. 'They're just having a nap, son.'

'We need to go.' Sabrinia poked her head out of the door. 'It's clear.' She turned back to the room.

Marlens pointed outside the room and above Sabrinia. She glanced at Bar Witch.

'Stop!' a Man-Hawk said.

Bar Witch swung her legs back into the cupboard and closed it. She peered through the gap.

The Man-Hawk walked into the room with its sword to Sabrinia's neck. 'You're all coming with me, or her head comes off.'

The others raised their hands. 'Whatever you want. Just don't hurt her,' Marlens said.

'Drop your weapons,' the Man-Hawk said.

Marlens glanced sideways at the cupboard. She dropped her dagger to the floor.

'Now kick everything into the corner of the room,' the Man-Hawk said.

Marlens removed her potion belt. She tapped a bottle of black smoke and tossed the belt onto the other weapons in the corner.

Bar Witch was on her own.

A HOPE IN HELL

Karl, stripped of his armour, bound and on his knees in the middle of the courtyard, faced Ryza and her mob of Man-Hawks and villains from across Hastovia.

Ryza approached Oaf and Quizmal. 'I want to thank you for bringing me back from the dead. Your reward is that you can die together.' She pointed to the top of the Lookout Tower at Death. 'Death! In a moment I'm going to command you to kill these people, and I don't want you to just touch their heads and dull their eyes. It's a bit boring. I want to see some slashes with the nails; maybe fly up high with someone then drop them so their bones smash. You know, make it a spectacle. Really show off your power and give it some variety. I have an audience to please.'

The other villains cheered.

Ryza reminded Karl of Arazod, desperate for showmanship, but somehow she was more irritating.

'Before that, though.' Ryza stepped towards Karl and grabbed his face. The heat stung his cheeks. 'I'm going to give Little General Arazod his revenge.' She turned to Arazod. 'You can kill this idiot and your wife.'

Karl expected Arazod's beak to curl into a smirk but it didn't.

'Consider this a thank you for your part in this, Little General Arazod,' Ryza said.

Arnul grabbed Karl and Sabrinia and dragged them to the well. They stood with their backs to it, but Karl expected they'd be in it soon enough. He wondered how many bodies were already down there.

Arazod stood in front of them. Ryza took the Soul Bleeder from Arnul and handed it to Arazod. He turned his axe in his hand and looked at them. 'I've missed my axe.'

'I can see why,' Sabrinia said. 'It can't talk back to tell you how horrible you are.'

Arazod's neck feathers twitched.

Karl looked up at the night. Peezant hovered up high.

Arazod glanced at Oaf.

'Just get it over with,' Karl told Arazod.

'I wish we'd left you to die!' Oaf said.

Sabrinia nudged Karl to look up at the Lookout Tower. Bar Witch poked her head out of the window.

'Little General Arazod. Get on with it,' Ryza said.

The Man-Hawks chanted his name.

Arazod stepped towards Karl and Sabrinia. He held his axe against Karl's neck but hesitated.

Ryza huffed. 'Arnul, this is boring. Get it done.'

Arnul approached Arazod and held his claw out. 'Give me the axe.'

A bleating caught everyone's attention. A bat-sheep with tiny wings shrieked its way down from the Lookout Tower window.

'What is that?' Arnul said.

Ryza scowled and shot fire at the creature, reducing it to ash.

'Little General Arazod?' Arnul waved his claw to hurry him along.

A horn sounded from beyond the west wall. A Fool emerged on top of the bricks. 'Attack!' the Fool yelled, and Fools flooded over Flowforn's walls.

Hope flooded Karl's body. Even if he died, there was hope for the others.

'Fools? Quick!' Arnul reached for the Soul Bleeder.

Arazod hacked Arnul's arm off then slashed his stomach. Arazod threw Arnul towards Karl and Sabrinia.

Sabrinia knocked Arnul into the well.

'Arazod!' Ryza yelled.

Marlens called up to the tower. 'The jar, Bar Witch!' A jar smashed and black smoke filled the courtyard.

'Death! Death! Get them all! Kill them!' Ryza commanded.

HIDING IN PLAIN SIGHT

Karl crawled and moved his arms around but was completely lost in the black smoke.

'Sabrinia!' he yelled, but there was no reply.

The smoke didn't make Karl cough, which was worse, heightening the blindness, the screams and the slashes. He hoped none of the screams would be from Sabrinia or his friends.

Shrieks came from above; the Man-Hawks must have been waiting to swoop in for the kill.

Karl crawled and his hand touched something fleshy. He groaned and crawled away from the sounds of steel clashing but a hand grabbed his ankle and he kicked out.

'Get off!' He drove his foot back.

'Stop Karl! It's me,' Frong said. 'Hold my ankle and follow.'

Karl turned and followed him. They crawled through a doorway and stayed low.

A Man-Hawk dropped and faced them. It opened its beak to shriek but a spear pierced its face.

Red flame burned through black smoke outside their hiding place. Screams echoed down the fire-covered alley.

Ryza probably burned her allies but didn't care.

'Stay quiet,' Frong said, their faces pressed to the wooden floor.

A black, ripped cloak stroked the pebbles outside. Steel boots turned and the toes pointed towards Karl and Frong.

'Death!' Ryza said. 'Are they dead?'

The feet vanished and appeared in front of Frong and Karl's faces. Karl trembled. One touch and he'd be dead.

Frong gripped Karl's wrist.

'No,' Death said. 'Even I cannot see through this smoke.' Death placed Karl's shield, a shazaq and Frong's spear in front of them, and then disappeared.

Karl and Frong looked at each other.

'Are you ready?' Frong said.

Karl nodded.

'For Larnela,' Frong said.

'For Sags. And all of us,' Karl replied.

They grabbed their weapons, got to their feet and ran through the smoke, adding their screams to the fight.

A CRUMBLING KINGDOM

Bar Witch struggled down the steps of the Lookout Tower, her energy sapped from creating the bat-sheep.

Her chest throbbed and she could barely carry the sword and everyone else's weapons. She ignored the battle grunts and approached the exit to the courtyard.

Smoke filled the tower. Bar Witch retreated and peered outside a window. About ten feet beneath her was a cart covered in straw.

'Physical exertion… Just what I need.' She threw Sabrinia's bow and arrows onto the cart, followed by Marlens' potions.

She leapt out of the window and crashed onto the straw. It didn't offer the padding she'd hoped for and the air left her lungs.

A flame from above ignited the alley and the heat stuck to her. She climbed to her feet and stumbled away. Flames flickered on debris.

She made her way to the wall that ran along the edge of the courtyard towards the tavern.

A Fool fell out of the smoke and stumbled onto its back.

A Man-Hawk followed and raised its sword to strike. The Fool blocked and sprung to its feet, but then a Cyclops woman leapt out of the smoke and squeezed the life out of the Fool.

The Man-Hawk and Cyclops woman turned to Bar Witch.

She barely had the strength to fight. She raised a sword and an arrow and dropped the other weapons. 'I know I'm dead, but I'm taking one of you with me. You can decide between you who that is or we could just get on with it.'

Her enemies charged.

Bar Witch drew her blade back, ready to swing. She hoped someone would free the Flowfornians from the tavern. 'Good luck to the rest of you.'

The Man-Hawk raised its sword but a dagger stuck into the side of its chest and it collapsed.

The Cyclops punched Bar Witch down and she rolled away from its stomp. The woman growing out of the beast's neck spat at Bar Witch and the Cyclops raised its fist but a shazaq pierced the beast's ribs and it fell.

Sabrinia dropped the sword.

Marlens stood above Bar Witch and extended a hand. Bar Witch pulled herself up.

Sabrinia took her bow and arrows. 'Thanks, Bar Witch.'

Marlens strapped her potion belt back on. 'Let's get to the gardens to get a bigger picture.'

'I have some idiots to check on first,' Bar Witch said. 'Good luck.'

She entered the tavern and opened the secret room. The relief on the faces of those she'd helped made her oddly proud.

'Right,' she said. 'There's a battle out there and it's a bit all over the place. So it's up to you. Outside the walls there are trees marked with circles that lead to a cart of supplies. You can run off and live in hiding, or stay and fight for your home.'

More people than she'd hoped ran off. 'Typical.'

'I'll help,' the annoying girl said.

Bar Witch smiled. She took the hair of the wizard-lizard, placed the abandoned baby on some straw and felt an emptiness about Hargon.

'I'll be back for you, little Alf.'

She closed the secret door and entered the battle.

PERILOUS PLAN

Oaf followed Arazod through the alleys. Although Arazod helped them, Oaf wanted to tear Arazod's arms off and whack him across the face with them.

Oaf squeezed Questions' and Quizmal's hands, worried Arazod could betray them and hand them over to Man-Hawks at any moment.

Arazod pointed to the back wall of the castle. 'Find a way out over there and keep going—' he wheezed. 'She won't be able to see you under the trees but that won't stop her burning everything.'

Oaf stared at him, confused by everything.

'Why did you save us?' Questions asked.

Arazod scratched his neck feathers and looked at Oaf. 'I... I don't know. But get your child somewhere safe.'

'I need to go back to help the others,' Oaf said.

Arazod shook his head. 'It won't work. She's a god now. She can't be killed by normal weapons or us—' he wheezed. 'So the best thing to do is to run and keep running.'

Oaf's body tensed. Karl's plan was doomed. 'Questions, you take Quizmal. I need to stop Karl.'

She grabbed his arm. 'What do you mean?'

'No time to explain.' Oaf pulled free and ran towards the battle. Arazod and Oaf's family called out to stop Oaf but he had to keep going.

THE HOPELESSNESS SCALE

The smoke cleared in the courtyard and the screams faded as the dead outnumbered the living. Karl blocked a sword and stabbed a Man-Hawk.

Death drove his nails into the chest of a Fool and then another. They didn't writhe or groan; their eyes simply turned greyer than their skin and they died.

A fireball whizzed past Karl and annihilated a Fool.

Ryza hovered above and fired more balls of death.

Karl rolled away from the heat.

One arrow hit Ryza in the ribs, then another.

Sabrinia and Marlens attacked from the garden entrance.

Ryza was unfazed. She pulled the arrows out of her body and sent a fireball towards Marlens and Sabrinia.

Karl stood below Ryza. 'Come and fight me. Prove you're the warrior you act like.'

She chuckled. 'Why should I waste my time with you?' She aimed her gauntlet and Karl's life flashed before his eyes in the fire forming around Ryza's fist.

An arrow exploded against her hand, knocking the gauntlet onto the pebbles and covering the air in smoke.

Marlens held a potion jar in her hand and Sabrinia celebrated next to her.

Karl readied his shazaq and waited for Ryza to fall out of the sky, but she flew down and slashed at Karl with her bladed wings, grazing his neck.

How did she survive that?

She flew at him again and sliced his ear.

She landed in front of him and swung the Grave Blade.

Karl lifted his shield but the impact shocked his forearm.

More arrows hit Ryza but hung off her body.

She swung again and again and Karl hid behind his shield. Karl had hoped to be more of a match but he couldn't mount an offence. Ryza was more powerful than before.

Oaf entered the courtyard. 'Karl! No!' He ran towards Karl.

'It's fine, Oaf!' he said.

Karl deflected a downward strike, knocking Ryza's blade to the side. He drew the shazaq back but couldn't thrust it forwards. The Grave Blade was wedged in his chest. He dropped his sword and his body lightened.

A grin stretched across Ryza's beak.

Oaf stopped.

'Karl!' Sabrinia yelled.

Marlens held Sabrinia back from charging at Ryza.

Karl tried to fight the agony but it flooded through him. He used all he had to smile at Ryza. 'I like how close we are.'

She twisted her sword. The smaller blades ripped Karl's insides.

Frong wedged his spear into Ryza's side, but it barely sunk in. 'How?'

Ryza turned to him and smirked. 'I'm a god now.' She elbowed him in the mouth, yanked the spear out and tossed it away.

Karl's fading heart tightened. The plan was meaningless. He looked at Sabrinia, grabbed a dagger from his belt and wedged it into Ryza's neck, but it snapped an inch into her skin.

She placed her talons against his chest. As she did with Sags, she kicked Karl off her sword as if he were an obstruction.

Karl flopped onto his back and stared at the stars.

'Hey! Want this?' Frong said to Ryza, holding the gauntlet.

Ryza flew after him, while Marlens and Sabrinia ran to Karl.

'Karl.' Sabrinia held his hands and cried. 'Can you do anything?' she asked Marlens.

Karl opened his hands and showed them the Soul of Illuminus he'd stolen from Ryza's neck. 'I can't outfight her but I outsmarted her.' He smiled through bloody teeth.

Sabrinia stroked his hair. 'We'll use it as soon as…' She bit her trembling lip.

'I understand now,' Karl said. 'What Illuminus was saying. Not life is death, but life is Death.' He cast a glance at the demon god, ending more lives.

'What are you talking about?' Sabrinia said.

'Death!' Karl held the orb. Ryza would realise it was missing. He had no time to tell Sabrinia everything he wanted.

'No, Karl!' She tried to pull the soul from his grip. 'We use it to command him. Then we use it to save you.'

'Illuminus' life isn't ours to use.' His grip loosened. 'Marlens, please.'

Marlens looked at him and cried. She took a potion bottle, opened it and stuck it under Sabrinia's nose, causing her to pass out. 'I'm sorry, Sabrinia.' Marlens stared at Karl.

'Thank you,' he said.

Marlens dragged Sabrinia and rested her among some barrels, away from the chaos.

Death appeared and floated parallel to Karl. He stared down through hollow, pain-filled eyes.

'There are less scary ways to arrive.' Karl held the Soul of Illuminus to Death's chest and it shone a stunning green.

Death lowered onto his feet and kneeled by Karl.

Illuminus' face appeared one last time and she smiled. 'Life is

Death.' The green orb disappeared and Illuminus formed in front of Karl. She stepped into Death's body and he glowed.

Death stood. He appeared full, alive, completely in the land of the living. 'Thank you.' A tear ran down his face.

Karl smiled and glanced towards the alleys.

Ryza flew around the corner. 'Where's my—' She saw Death and flew away.

Karl touched Death's foot. 'Help them fix things, please.'

Death nodded and ran into battle.

Marlens lifted Karl under the arms and dragged him towards the gardens. 'Come on, pal.' She choked back tears.

'Where does me surviving land on the hopelessness scale?'

Marlens sniffled and chuckled.

'Thought as much,' Karl said.

'Nothin' you've ever done has been hopeless,' she said. 'I was able to give Sags a few more moments. Let's do the same for you, old chum.'

AN HONEST CHOICE

Sabrinia awoke among barrels. Ahead of her Death stood with Fools destroying Man-Hawks, Cyclops women and turning the tide in Flowforn's favour.

Karl...

She rose to her feet, grabbed her weapons and ran back to where she last saw him. Maybe he was still alive. Hopefully. He had to be.

Ryza landed in the courtyard, Quizmal in her grasp. 'Stop!' she yelled at everyone.

The battle halted and everyone watched her.

'Quizmal!' Oaf said, looking for Questions.

'All of you in a bunch!' Ryza commanded, backing towards the wall under the Lookout Tower.

The Flowfornians, Fools, Death and the others all stood where she demanded. Sabrinia stood behind Frong and Oaf. Where were Marlens and Karl?

Ryza placed the Grave Blade to Quizmal's neck. 'Give me the gauntlet or I shred his little neck.'

Frong stepped forward and threw it to her.

'Death,' Sabrinia whispered and held the arrow with the rune markings to him. 'Can you charge this with your power?'

Death aimed those terrifying hollows in his head at her. He placed his scaly hand on her wrist, turned her wrist to face the sky and ran his nail along her palm, drawing blood. 'You can do it yourself.'

Sabrinia held the arrow in her bloody hand and the rune markings glowed. What was going on?

Ryza put the gauntlet on and took aim at them. 'You all think you are good but you're no better than me. You kill to protect your people, and all I've ever done is kill to further the Man-Hawks.'

Sabrinia took aim and stepped forward. It was too risky. If Ryza moved Quizmal he'd be dead. 'The only killing we've done is when we've been attacked,' Sabrinia said.

'So have I!' Ryza said. 'Father told me of a time Man-Hawks lived peacefully, but it was humans, jealous of our ability to fly who tried to clip our wings.'

Sabrinia raised a hand. 'You can't blame all humans for the stupid actions of a few. Much like we can't dismiss all Man-Hawks as evil.' Sabrinia placed her bow and arrow on the pebbles. 'If you give us Quizmal, we can discuss a way to live together, to help each other and end the conflict.'

A wounded Man-Hawk limped out of the alleys. 'I like the sound of that.'

Ryza looked at the Man-Hawk. 'History will only repeat itself. Shared power doesn't work. Beings need someone they can look up to, to respect, to fear. It's the only way.'

'We can change that,' Sabrinia said.

Ryza scoffed. 'Gods don't need to make deals with people. You can all burn with your wretched home.' Flames covered her arm around Quizmal and he screeched.

'Quizmal!' Oaf yelled and ran towards them.

Ryza aimed her arm towards Oaf.

Arazod leapt from a window in the tower and landed on her.

Oaf ran to his son and pulled him out of harm's way.

Arazod grabbed Ryza and pushed her against the wall.

'Shoot her,' Frong said to Sabrinia.

'I can't. Not with Arazod there,' she said.

Ryza pecked Arazod's shoulder. 'You idiot, Little Arazod. You've cost me everything!' She pecked him again and again, tearing at him. She tried to spread her wings but he held them down.

'Sabrinia. Do it!' Arazod cried through the pain. Ryza pecked the meat off his shoulders and flames covered her body.

Arazod's screeches would haunt Sabrinia for however long she lived.

'Please, Sabrinia. It's the only chance,' Arazod shrieked. 'I'll only betray you again. It's in me.' His feathers darkened and his claws reddened.

Sabrinia lifted her weapon and released the arrow. It wedged the siblings together and they fell to the floor, joined in death. With her last breaths, Ryza pecked at Arazod again and again.

ONE LIFE

Sabrinia punched Marlens in the face and she took it. 'Why? Why did you let him?'

Frong held Sabrinia back. 'It's what he wanted.'

Karl stretched his arm out. 'Do you really want to say goodbye like this?'

Sabrinia kneeled by Karl and grabbed his head. 'You idiot.'

He smiled. 'That's me.' He placed his hands on her face. He wanted to feel that warmth and take in the glow of her eyes one last time.

'We could've used the orb to command Death and then revive you,' Sabrinia said.

'But it's not ours to use.' Karl looked at Death who nodded.

'Is there anything you can do?' Sabrinia asked Death.

Death shook his head. 'I can help him to pass without pain.'

'That'd be nice. I am in a fair bit of agony right now.' Karl coughed. 'Ryza's sword is really, really awful.'

Oaf, Questions and Quizmal approached.

'Will I miss you?' Questions said, tears in her eyes.

'I'll miss you too, Questions,' Karl said. 'Remember to put that cage around the pool of tortured souls,' Karl told Oaf.

Oaf nodded. 'If you turn into a ghost, come and visit us from time to time, but not in a spooky way.'

'Of course I will.' Karl chuckled, his throat tight.

Quizmal cried and hugged his mum. 'Bye Uncle Karl.'

Karl smiled at him.

The trio left Frong and Marlens to say their goodbyes.

Frong held Karl's hand. 'If there's a way to bring you back, know we'll find it.'

Karl shook his head. 'Don't worry about that. I've had a good go at this life.'

Marlens pulled on her hair. 'Sorry I couldn't save you.'

'Stop it. You both made my life better. Frong, promise me you'll visit my grave and tell me long and boring stories from time to time.'

He choked up. 'I promise.'

Marlens and Frong left Karl and Sabrinia alone.

His body ached. 'You were right. We never get enough time with the ones we love.'

She nodded. 'Sorry we were never bound.'

He shook his head. 'We didn't need a ceremony. It's here.' He touched his heart.

Sabrinia bit her lip. 'I love you.'

'I love you too.' He took a breath. 'Time to go now.'

She kissed his lips and he felt alive one last time.

He stroked her hair. 'Good luck and be careful...'

They finished the sentence together, 'It's a strange world out there.'

Sabrinia hung her head.

Death touched Karl's forehead. Everything around him peeled away and the faces of those who had given him meaning faded. His world turned green and he was on the shore where he had seen Illuminus, only she wasn't there this time. The green sea swirled around his feet and a sense of calm came over him.

The layers fell and the green crumbled into darkness and screams.

NEW LIFE IN DEATH

A sunset passed and the air was still heavy with sadness, particularly in Flowforn's cemetery where they gathered. Sabrinia wished the tears would stop, but something broke within her and it would be a while before it repaired.

Oaf touched the hair of the wizard-lizard to Arazod's back. His wings returned with red and blue feathers.

'I know it's raw right now,' Oaf said. 'But he's proof that there's good in everyone. Somewhere.'

Sabrinia nodded.

Oaf jumped into the grave and laid Arazod to rest. He placed the Soul Bleeder in Arazod's claws. The Man-Hawk would be buried among Flowfornians.

Oaf shovelled soil on top of him.

Karl's grave was next to Larnela's; mother and son reunited.

Sags' grave was next to theirs, although his body wouldn't be in it. The hair didn't work at restoring Sags' form, but Frong kept his hand in a satchel. People would find it strange, but Frong didn't care.

Proster's death stone rested under a tree. They never recovered Hargon but placed his death stone next to Proster's.

Sabrinia approached Death.

'There's more to you than you know,' he told her. 'I suggest you travel to the northern islands – find out more about your parents.'

'But my mother and father were from the south.'

Death shook his head. 'No. The guardians they left you with were. You are more than this castle and your people. Go and seek your true roots.'

He could've given her that news less bluntly. 'Why should I believe you?'

Death stared at her. 'It's up to you. Stay and wait for the next evil, always reacting, or go and become the force to prevent it. You're not as heroic as you think. Neither are you as weak as you fear.'

Her life was dedicated to the people. Leaving them in their time of rebuilding would be selfish and she had no idea if she could trust a god. They were known for manipulating people, not helping them. She thought it best to change the subject. 'Arazod, if you're here, bound to me, thank you for what you did. If you're not, then – well, I'm talking to the wind.'

Death chuckled. 'Bound souls? That's all nonsense. A story invented to stop people behaving like animals. He is now in the Realm of the Dead.'

It was bittersweet. She wished she'd married Karl.

'We'll help you to rebuild, Sabrinia, then you can decide what you want to do,' Frong said.

It was all a bit much, the thought that her father wasn't her father. It made her think about all the signs. She realised his lack of affection wasn't because he was worried about tragedy, but perhaps because she was a burden he was protecting.

'I'm thinking of heading north,' Marlens said. 'There's an alchemist who knows how to raise the dead. If he's alive I want to learn from him.'

'I'll help you,' Death said. 'I sense a god there. The sooner I rid the world of the others, the better. And now I can no longer cross between realms they will sense me too and come out of hiding.'

Frong scratched his beard. 'How about before we rush into any decisions we grab a drink? Death, I'm sure now you're in the land of the living there are things you want to try.'

'Well, yes. I've always wondered what it would be like to have a nap, and perhaps an ale would make my insides feel a little less empty.'

'Then it's settled. We won't make a decision on our next steps until we are suitably drunk,' Frong said.

'Plus Bar Witch needs a hand looking after that kid,' Marlens said.

'I'll follow,' Sabrinia said.

They walked away.

Sabrinia returned to Karl's grave and sat in front of his stone. She thought about Ryza and felt guilty. People craving power often drove innocents to extremes and pulled them into their way of living. If Ryza was telling the truth, her people were victims too of some evil before. Sabrinia had to find a way for good to get to people before evil did. It was an infection that spread by using weakness and fear, but Arazod proved there was always good in people.

She left the cemetery and joined the others in the Adventurer Tavern.

Frong and Death chatted away and ate stew while Bar Witch served a customer. Sabrinia approached the side of the bar and lifted Alf from his cot. He wept.

'Oh no,' Bar Witch said. 'It took me ages to get him to sleep. I'll have to give him some ale now.'

Sabrinia glared at Bar Witch.

'I'm joking!' Bar Witch took Alf and made bizarre noises. 'It's what Hargon did.'

Sabrinia placed a hand on Bar Witch's shoulder. 'I'm sorry.'

Bar Witch shrugged. 'What can we do? At least we have his art to remind us of him.'

Sabrinia scanned the paintings. So vivid. There was the time Karl was in the dungeon, then when Arazod was in the dungeon, and the painting of Sabrinia firing the arrow at the dummy. Then there was a bizarre painting of Hargon but it was awful.

'I did that one,' Bar Witch said. 'Not got his skills but they say it's about the meaning.'

Sabrinia chuckled and took in a song from the troupe of tree people. They should've been playing their violins at Sags and Frong's wedding, not at a mass funeral. One of the tree people tapped her feet, kicking up a jolly rhythm.

> *Life is a road on the path to death,*
> *Better make it fun,*
> *Savour every breath.*
> *There are twists and turns along the way,*
> *To find meaning,*
> *But it'll never delay.*
> *It's coming! It's coming! Death is coming for you!*
> *It's coming! It's coming! So give meaning to all you do!*

Death stood up and sang along.

> *'Death's coming! Death's coming! So live a life that's*
> *true!'*

Sabrinia smiled at Marlens and Frong and left, not in the mood.

She searched the debris of the King's Tower in the courtyard and found the wreckage of her old room. She opened the crate of Karl's belongings and held his tatty shirt and wept.

She saw an old book, *For Sabrinia,* and opened it. She smiled through the tears. It was all of the three-word monsters they'd conjured up in their imaginations. There were her favourites, the flaming donkey sloth, the hollow bread bat, the leaf-headed ant woman. The drawings were terrible but that made them all the more beautiful.

She closed the book and held it to her chest. She gazed at the sky. She'd never imagined leaving her people, but her adventure was only beginning.

THE END

EPILOGUE

*M*ud filled Karl's mouth. He coughed and grasped at anything until he felt a rock. He grabbed it and pulled himself out of the muddy pit and onto what felt like sharp stones.

Screams echoed around him.

He coughed mud out, wiped it from his eyes and caught his breath. He sat up.

What was going on? The last thing he remembered was Death touching him. Had Death sent him to hell?

Karl touched his bare chest and wiped mud off it. The wound from the Grave Blade was gone. It was as if he were healed, but for what? To suffer again?

Fire burned in the distance.

Karl walked towards it but a red sword hovered and blocked his path. He took another step but the sword pointed at him.

That was enough of a warning. 'I guess I'll go the other way.' He turned and faced a long rocky path he could easily fall off.

'Great.' Karl spotted a dead man dangling over the edge of the path. He pulled him up and nearly threw up.

The man's face had been scratched and his chest shredded.

His eyes were missing. Why had Karl been sent here? When could he finally rest?

Karl spotted what he assumed was the man's dagger in the distance. He picked it up.

Beyond a mountain, cheers erupted and a puff of fire rose.

Karl continued and a ghostly figure in scratched armour walked towards him. Karl stopped and so did she. Her dark hair clung to her face like a net and her bloody smile shook his soul.

She beckoned him with her finger, but Karl froze. He wanted nothing to do with her.

She folded her arms and two half human, half bats emerged from behind her and perched on her shoulders. They screeched and looked hungry.

She beckoned Karl once again. 'I don't need another warning.' He walked towards her, terrified of what awaited. He would have to earn his rest.

THE RISE OF RAGNUS

WELCOME PARTY

*A*udyn stood in the doorway of his and his mother's three-room shack. He smiled as the first streaks of sunrise stroked his quiet little village of Gemeria.

He inhaled the invigorating, earthy air and tapped his boots against the mud. He slipped slightly, but was confident the grip would be good enough to get to the potato fields for the harvest.

Audyn had helped his mother with harvesting for the last two years, since he had turned seven and his father had disappeared.

It was his favourite time of year for the fun he had with his mother, but one steeped in sadness at the thought of being abandoned.

Audyn adored his village and the hill it stood on, overlooking the plains of Lansino. To Audyn, this was the finest place in all of Hastovia, even though he hadn't seen anywhere beyond the potato fields that were a short walk from his door. There could be joyous mysteries out there, such as singing rocks, flying trees, or horses made of grass, but he didn't care. This was all he needed.

So what if Gemeria got so muddy when it rained that if he stood in one place for too long he could sink?

So what if there were only five little shacks, and entertainment was so limited it involved rocks, sticks and mud?

So what if he had to always pick spider-worms out of his bed? After a while they became a feature of the shacks, and Audyn would even speak to them as friends.

He'd overheard other villagers talk about the kingdom of Romoro, a sunset's walk north of Gemeria, but the main things that they mentioned were people gambling, arranged marriages, drinking and the finest warriors.

Boring, boring, boring.

Audyn wouldn't trade his village for the city. His mother had told him that people became selfish in cities, worried about coin above community.

Romoro did seem popular, though, as the only time anyone passed by Gemeria would be to have a toilet break on their way to the city. The Gemerians had become fed up with the frequent toilet visitors, so they built a toilet shack specifically for passers-by. Audyn had thought people might be stopping to sample their potatoes, the most delicious potatoes in the land, but nobody ever did. He would make sure anyone who stopped in Gemeria left knowing all about the potatoes, though, and how they grew in blessed soil.

He wanted to share the potatoes with everyone and he couldn't wait to collect this latest batch before the cold season arrived.

Audyn rolled his shoulders and stretched his calves and hamstrings. Last year he had forgotten to, and after all that digging and bending he had spent the following days waddling like a groggy ogre.

He grabbed the pitchfork that rested against the doorframe and spun it in his hands. He couldn't wait to sink it into the mud and dig up that first potato plant. He loved the sound of the forks piercing the soil.

'Ma! Come on!' Eighty-three sunsets they'd waited for a fresh batch of potatoes. The whole village was excited.

'The potatoes aren't going anywhere, Audyn,' she said from inside then emerged from the shack, wearing a thick brown top and mud-stained trousers. She dropped a sack and a shovel at the entrance, leaned over and planted a kiss on Audyn's forehead.

He admired how powerful and muscular she was. Out of Gemeria's five inhabitants, she was by far the strongest. Audyn wanted to be as strong as her when he grew up, but his arms were still as thin as the pitchfork's shaft.

'Boots,' she said.

Audyn placed a hand against the doorframe and showed her the soles of his boots.

'You'll need a better grip, my love. Get the spiked soles otherwise you'll be sliding to the fields.' She smiled and pushed her brown hair behind her ear.

'Thanks, Ma.' He ran in, changed into the boots with spiked soles and returned.

'Ready?' she asked.

He nodded, grabbed his mother's hand and squeezed it. She was the best.

They walked towards the potato fields but a commotion caught Audyn's mother's attention. By the well, two old people and a small girl, all covered in slashed rags and mud, spoke to Rowtes, the village elder and his two friends Nucri and Gurm. Rowtes had the usual look of misery on his face, while Nucri and Gurm had the usual looks of not knowing very much.

The visitors probably needed the toilet. If they'd shown up slightly later they could've had a potato.

As Audyn neared he noticed the old people crying and the girl distressed. A sack was on the mud between them.

Rowtes folded his arms. 'I don't care. Leave,' he barked out of his eternally dismissive mouth.

Gurm nodded and Nucri chewed his bottom lip.

Audyn thought Nucri should eat more. Then he wouldn't have to eat his face so much.

The old lady fell to her knees. 'Please. My child needs to rest.'

The girl coughed and held her throat. Her light hair was so thin it blew around in the wind like smoke.

Rowtes reached into his pocket and took out a sharp stone. He held it threateningly. 'I said leave.'

The girl cried and Audyn turned to his mother. 'Why can't we help them? They can rest in my room.'

Gurm took a swig of his ale and dropped his tankard on the mud. Audyn picked it up, as he often found himself doing, to keep Gemeria clean.

Rowtes turned to Audyn's mother. 'Shut your kid up, Padel.'

She stood in front of Audyn. 'Maybe if you answered his question it would help him to understand.'

The girl's cough sounded like it was ripping her throat.

Rowtes stared at Audyn's mother in that creepy way Audyn had seen over the years. 'I'm not risking someone coming from Romoro and seeing this filth here. They'll take one look at them and leave.'

Apart from their torn rags, Audyn couldn't see much of a difference between the people and themselves.

Audyn's mother scoffed. 'It doesn't matter how many begging letters you send, Rowtes. Nobody from Romoro is coming.'

'They will come! And when they taste our potatoes they will welcome us into their kingdom and we can finally leave this muddy hell behind.'

Audyn's mother laughed. 'Why are you so desperate to enter Romoro? Is it because an arranged marriage is the only way you'll ever get someone to lay with you?'

Audyn chuckled and noticed Gurm bite his finger to hold his laugh in. Rowtes turned to Gurm whose face became more serious.

'Very funny,' Rowtes said, but his face showed no signs of humour. He turned to the family. 'I won't tell you again.'

The old woman looked at Audyn's pitchfork. 'What if we help you to work? My daughter can rest while we work for you.'

Rowtes scowled. 'I don't want your dirty hands anywhere near our potatoes. You'll probably infect them.'

Audyn squeezed his mother's hand and looked up at her. 'Ma, you always say kindness brings kindness. Why can't we be kind to them?'

Audyn's mother looked at the girl and Audyn noticed the sadness in his mother's eyes.

'Word spreads, Rowtes,' Audyn's mother said.

'What?'

'If these people find somewhere else to stay and then tell of how you treated them, maybe Romoro will hear of it and won't be so accepting of you. I'm sure a Romoran would rather invite those who help into their kingdom, ahead of those who abuse.'

Rowtes' brow narrowed.

The old people looked at each other and the woman spoke. 'If you turn us away I will tell whoever I can of you, Rowtes. Rowtes the Abusive. Rowtes the Rotten.'

Rowtes turned to Gurm and Nucri. They shrugged.

Rowtes put his stone back in his pocket and pointed at Audyn's mother. 'Fine. You tell them what needs doing.' He dismissively waved the back of his hand at them.

Audyn smiled up at his mother, proud to be her son.

'Hold on,' Rowtes said. He took a couple of steps towards the old couple. 'What's in the sack?'

The old woman looked to her husband who opened the sack and showed Rowtes several bottles of wine and juice.

The woman picked one up. 'Some wine and juice my family made. We have been to collect it at the ceremony of their passing.'

'Give us all of that,' Rowtes demanded.

The woman shook her head. 'We can't. It's…we need to sell it, to improve our situation.'

'I don't care about your situation. I care about mine.'

Audyn's mother pulled Audyn's hand and they walked next to the old couple.

'Just leave them alone, Rowtes,' Audyn's mother said. She turned to the couple and child. 'Come with us.' She led them all back to Audyn's shack.

Rowtes called after them. 'Sort your kid out then come and do something useful.'

The old couple bowed to Audyn and his mother. 'I am Sabata,' the woman said and then pointed to the man. 'And this is Uldeen. Our angel is Agra.'

'I hope she is okay,' Audyn's mother said.

Finally, they could dig.

Audyn's mother stirred the potato stew and hummed while Audyn watched, mesmerised by how peaceful she looked. After a long day of digging, this was the perfect way to relax.

Sabata stood in the doorway to Audyn's shack, dressed in his mother's gown and she watched everyone, while Rowtes and his friends loaded a cart with sacks of potatoes. They only stopped to drink more ale.

Rowtes approached Audyn's mother. 'You might be right and Romoro might never come,' he slurred.

Audyn's mother shrugged, not bothering to look up at Rowtes.

He moved closer and stood over her as she stirred the stew. 'Tomorrow, I'm taking this to Romoro and getting out of this dump. There's enough potatoes left for you and your runt.'

Audyn looked at the shed where there was one saggy sack of potatoes left.

'Good luck to you,' Audyn's mother said, never looking up from stirring.

Rowtes smirked and walked back to his friends.

Audyn wiped soil off his face. It was all over him. In his ears and up his nose, but he loved it. His arms ached from all the digging.

Sabata and her family joined them.

'Can I help?' Sabata asked.

Audyn's mother smiled. 'You can pass me the carnat fungus from that bucket.'

'Carnat fungus?' Sabata winced, taking a handful of the red mushrooms.

Audyn's mother chuckled. 'You just need to know how to prepare them to kill the bitterness. Audyn?'

He took the hard mushrooms from Sabata and placed them on a shovel blade. He held it over the fire until the red blackened and then pulled the shovel away from the fire. His mother handed him a knife and he made an incision along the stipe of each mushroom. He squeezed the stipe over some bread, allowing a syrup-like fluid to drop onto it.

He handed the moist bread to Sabata.

She apprehensively took a bite. 'It's sweet!' She passed it to Uldeen who took a bite and smiled, still not saying a word.

Audyn prepared another handful of mushrooms and his mother tossed the caps into the pot of stew. She served everyone bowls of stew and Rowtes ate his as soon as it was in his hands. He slurped and spilled it all over himself.

After the meal, Sabata stood. 'I'd like to thank you all.'

'Shut up,' Rowtes said.

'Rowtes!' Audyn's mother barked. 'Go on, Sabata.'

'We will never forget your kindness. And while we didn't want to give you our wine and juice earlier, we realised that it would be shameful to sell it. It was made by my parents with the intention to share, so we cannot bring shame on our family. We would like to share it with you.'

'Good. Get me a cup then and don't be tight with how much you fill it,' Rowtes said.

Sabata and Uldeen went into the shack and returned with several bottles. They poured wine for the adults, and Audyn was given a cup of sickly sweet grape juice.

Rowtes raised a cup. 'To mine and my friends' new life that starts tomorrow!'

The three men cheered.

Audyn's mother unenthusiastically raised her cup and took a sip.

Audyn hoped Romoro took the men in so he wouldn't have to see them ever again.

Audyn's mother wrapped her arms around Audyn. 'Please never be like them.'

Audyn pulled away and smiled at her. 'I won't.' He broke eye contact and gazed at the mud. The family unit of Sabata, Uldeen and Agra made him miss the closeness of a full family. 'You've always told me that kindness brings good things, but if it does...' He had to ask. 'Then why did Father leave?' He couldn't look at her in case his question had made her sad.

His mother stroked his head and pulled him into her chest. 'Maybe it was a good thing he left.'

It wasn't the answer he had wanted, but he guessed it would have to do. His mother let him go. 'Being kind has given me you. And you're the best thing in Hastovia.'

He smiled. 'You are!'

The grown ups seemed to relax a lot more as they gulped the wine. Then his mother said the words Audyn loved to hear.

'Who wants to have a mud sliding contest?'

He instantly took up the challenge, as did Rowtes, who held the record for sliding the length of fifteen planks of wood.

'Sabata? Uldeen?' Audyn's mother asked.

They looked at each other and Sabata joined them.

Audyn's mother lined up twenty planks and marked a starting line in the soil. Audyn went first. He took his top off to reduce the resistance, stared at the mud, took a breath, and sprinted with all his power. He approached the line in the soil and dived chest-first onto the mud. He slid and held his arms and legs off the ground to keep his speed up. He came to a stop, stood and counted. Ten planks. An improvement on his last record of nine. His chest was covered in mud and he didn't bother to wipe it off. He loved how it felt and rubbed it over his body.

Rowtes went next. 'Here comes another record.' He ran up, and even though he was slightly swaying, he slid as far as sixteen planks. He stood up, bowed, then walked back to his friends while tensing so hard he might explode.

It was Sabata's turn. She removed the gown and laughed all the way from her run up to end of her slide. She only managed eight planks, but she clearly had a great time. She wiped the mud off her chest with a cloth and put the gown back on.

Audyn's mother was the last to slide. 'Rowtes. When you leave tomorrow, you'll be leaving a loser.' She took a run up and Audyn could see the determination in her eyes. She leapt, slid on her chest, and when she stopped and stood she'd made it to eighteen planks.

Audyn leapt and ran over to her. 'The mud sliding champion is my mother, Padel!'

Rowtes shook her hand. 'I would've won if I wasn't so drunk. And now, I'm going to get more drunk. Give me more of that wine!'

The grown ups finished another bottle of wine and Audyn watched his muddy mother smile and dance with Sabata and Uldeen. He wished he could freeze this moment. He'd not seen her smile like this since his father had left. Sure there had been moments, but this looked different, less like she was trying to smile and more like the smile wanted to be there.

Rowtes stumbled and fell into the stew pot, knocking the left-overs over.

Audyn's mother huffed and shook her head. 'What an idiot.'

Rowtes didn't make any comment or get up, though.

Audyn drank another cup of juice, and as the night sun rose the day's activities caught up with him and his body weakened.

He glanced over at Sabata and Uldeen. They stopped dancing and walked to the edge of the circle. Their smiles had gone and they looked sad. Maybe they were tired too.

Audyn's head felt light. He took a step towards a stool but his legs wobbled. 'Ma?'

He turned to her, but she became a blur. A blur that fell to the mud.

Audyn's mouth dried and he strained. 'Ma...' He dropped his cup and fell.

THE BLAME GAME

udyn woke up staring at the thatch of the roof. It took him a moment to realise he was on the floor of his shack and on his mother's lap. His head throbbed as if he'd been violently shaken.

'You're okay!' His mother held him to her chest and kissed his head. 'Thank Mother Hastovia that you're okay!' She released him and they both shuffled to the wall and sat up against it.

'What happened?' he asked.

She held him in a seated position. 'I don't know.' She poured water into his mouth and it filled every part of him as though he were empty.

He coughed and the smell of yesterday's grape juice filled the air. 'Everything hurts, Ma.' He closed his eyes for a moment and his mother squeezed him.

They stepped outside of the shack and the cart was gone, evident by its tracks disappearing into the distance. Audyn assumed it meant Rowtes and his friends were gone, but then he noticed Rowtes smash a stool against the side of his home.

'They've taken it all!' He stomped up to Audyn's mother and poked his finger into her face. 'It's your fault and that little idiot.' His face was red and his teeth showing. 'I'll never be part of Romoro!'

'Hey!' Audyn's mother moved Audyn behind her. 'Potatoes or no potatoes, they wouldn't take you. And those thieves. They'll get to the gates of Romoro, the potatoes will be taken off them, and they'll be turned away or slaughtered. Exactly what would've happened to you, so count yourself lucky.'

'Lucky! Lucky!' He bashed his fist against the side of their shack. 'I'm more than this dump!' He placed his hand in his pocket.

Gurm and Nucri stood by Rowtes.

'You don't even deserve this place,' Audyn's mother said.

Rowtes stepped up to her and the smell of stale ale lingered.

'Leave her!' Audyn stood as tall as he could by his mother's side. Rowtes grabbed Audyn's head and whacked it off the shack's wood. Pain shot through Audyn's skull and he fell, grabbing his head in the hope he could squeeze the pain away.

Audyn's mother punched Rowtes and then threw him onto the mud. 'Don't ever touch him!' She tended to Audyn, but Gurm and Nucri grabbed her arms. She pushed them away too, then reached an arm to Audyn to help him up. 'Are you okay, my love?'

Audyn spotted Rowtes take the stone out of his pocket. 'Ma!'

Rowtes thumped the stone against the back of her head.

'No!' Audyn leapt for Rowtes, but Nucri and Gurm grabbed him.

THE WORST KIND OF SHOW

'Stop it!' Audyn cried. He tried to break free of the ropes wrapped around his wrists and ankles.

His mother hung upside down from a chain, attached to a wooden beam running along Rowtes' storage room.

Rowtes whacked her face with the stone. Blood covered her cheeks and dripped onto the wooden floorboards.

Gurm and Nucri cleared the furniture out of the room.

'Don't look,' Audyn's mother begged Audyn, but he had to.

'Let her go!' he yelled. 'Please!'

Rowtes walked over to Audyn and tossed the bloody stone up and caught it. Rowtes wiped the stone on Audyn's top, leaving a bloody streak. He booted Audyn in the stomach, then returned to Audyn's mother and squeezed her damaged face. 'If I have to accept the misery of my life, so do you.'

Rowtes released her chain and she crashed head-first against the wooden floor. He left her in a heap on the floorboards. He exited the room.

'Please close your eyes,' Audyn's mother strained. 'Please, my love. I'll be okay.'

He couldn't break free. He grunted and yelled but it made no difference.

'Please…' she said again, her breaths big and slow.

'I want to help you, Ma.'

'No,' she said. 'We have to be patient.'

Laughter carried into the room. Audyn blamed himself. If he hadn't made his mother help the people she'd be okay. How could people he thought of so fondly do that to them? How could kindness lead to the worst kind of awfulness?

Nucri entered and dragged Audyn's mother's chained body to the opposite wall from Audyn. She stared at Audyn and he understood she waned him to stay quiet.

Gurm followed and he nailed a hook, high up to the wall. He left.

Nucri stood Audyn's mother up, tied a chain around her neck and secured her to the hook. Her limp body hung off it and her legs barely kept her upright.

Nucri left and returned with some bottles and bandages. He poured one of the liquids onto a bandage and dabbed Audyn's mother's face. She winced and closed her eyes.

Audyn was relieved she was being helped, though.

'Please help Audyn,' she asked. 'Do what you want to me, but he's only a boy.'

Nucri ignored her. He took some thread and a needle and stitched the gash under her cheek.

Audyn remembered his mother stitching him when he tried to spin the spading fork in his hands and it sliced his thigh. Did this mean she was going to be okay?

'Are you going to free us, Nucri?' Audyn asked.

Nucri remained silent and cleaned more of Audyn's mother's face, and when she was a mess of stitches and bandages he picked up his things and stopped in the doorway.

He turned back to Audyn's mother. 'You know. I always wanted to live in the city. Not like Rowtes for the women or the drinking. I wanted a house of stone. I wanted access to all the stone they had there, to carve stone figures and sell them at the market. I might've become famous, with my stone-carved figures in houses all the way up the Kolada river.'

'You still can be,' Audyn's mother said. 'There is stone everywhere.'

'Not Romoran stone.' Nucri shook his head. 'You've wrecked that dream. And we're going to remind you every day.' He left.

THE REWARD FOR KINDNESS

The routine continued for more sunsets than Audyn could remember. First came the sound of footsteps, followed by Audyn's mother being hung upside down and then beaten with that horrible stone Rowtes had.

Rowtes would kiss the stone then smash her face. The other two would punch her body, then they'd heal her again to repeat it the next sunset.

Audyn had never heard so many crunches or seen people take such joy in someone else's misery. The only food Audyn and his mother ate was one section of a potato a sunset, and a cup of muddy water. The closest thing to a wash was a bucket of cold muddy water tossed over them.

The footsteps were the only way Audyn could tell it was a new sunrise. He wasn't free from the beatings either. He'd take a few kicks from them, to remind him he was nothing.

They beat Audyn's mother again, then unchained her from the beam and secured her to the hook. They left.

'Please don't watch, Audyn,' she said.

He wanted to close his eyes every time, but he had to watch, to see if there was a moment, anything he could use to try to free them.

His mother had given only kindness to the world, and her thanks, this.

Audyn shuffled back against the wooden wall and rubbed the ropes against it.

'Audyn, don't try anything. They will get fed up and leave us. I promise.'

He stared at her and felt around the wooden planks. He ran his fingers over a nail and just about got his fingernail under it. It hurt and felt like it could pull his fingernail off, but this was his only hope.

As the daily beatings and healings continued he was able to close his eyes, because he had his plan. As long as he kept his hands safe he didn't care which part of his body they pummelled.

Audyn's mother's face became further disfigured. She looked less like his mother every time and it scared him. The swelling buried her eyes and her lips looked like they could burst. She was a mess of purple and yellow bruising, as though her usual colour wanted to leave her face to escape the pain.

After several more sunsets of beatings the nail was loose and Audyn scratched it against his ropes to loosen them. A few more sunsets and one morning he pulled them loose.

'No, Audyn. Don't do it,' his mother begged.

'I have to.' It was his fault they were here, and he would get them out. He thought about pulling the plank off the wall and creating an opening they could escape through, but he needed the key to unchain his mother. He'd have to kill the three men.

'I beg you, my love.' In her eyes there was still life. Still hope.

Audyn shook his head and her hope faded just enough for him to know he'd hurt her. She'd be okay when he freed her.

The footsteps neared again, and no matter how many times it happened, his heart still raced and his mind wondered whether today was the day he and his mother would die.

The men dished out the usual dose of abuse, but today Audyn absorbed it all, knowing he would give it back.

Nucri was on his own again, healing Padel. She watched Audyn move, removing the ropes from his wrists and untying his legs.

'Describe my face to me, Nucri,' Audyn's mother asked.

'What?'

'I can't remember what I look like. And you've done so much to my appearance I'd like to know what I look like now. How would you describe me?'

He stopped dabbing her face.

Audyn took careful steps on the wooden planks, willing them to not creak.

Nucri scratched his head. 'Erm…you look like someone should never have to look.' Nucri shook his head. 'I'm sorry.'

Audyn wrapped his left arm around Nucri's neck and with his right hand he jammed the nail into Nucri's eye. Nucri's shriek echoed through the room.

Audyn stabbed him again and again all over his face, until blood poured out of several pin holes.

Audyn picked up the ropes that had bound him and wrapped them around Nucri's neck. he struggled and flailed around, but Audyn fell back against the wall.

Nucri elbowed Audyn, over and over, but Audyn took it and the elbow strikes weakened.

Nucri passed out.

'Audyn, the keys,' his mother said.

Audyn fumbled for Nucri's keys and reached for his mother's lock, but Rowtes and Gurm ran in.

'The bottles. Hit them!' Audyn's mother said.

Audyn swung a medicine bottle at Gurm, but Rowtes caught his wrist and whacked it off the wall. Audyn dropped the bottle and it smashed off the wood.

He fought and fought, but after a blur of screams and kicks, everything was black again.

Audyn woke up chained and back where he was before. There was no way out this time. He struggled against the restraints but only hurt himself.

Rowtes and Gurm grinned at him.

'You did some damage to our friend.' Rowtes shook his head. 'When he's okay I'm sure he'll want to have a chat with you.' Rowtes booted Audyn's stomach and spat on him. 'It would be harsh to blame you, though, you're only a kid.' Rowtes turned to Audyn's mother. 'I put it down to a poor upbringing.'

Rowtes and Gurm walked over to Audyn's mother.

'All I've ever wanted was to break free of the peasant's life. To change the path I was born on. To have a wife,' Rowtes told her. 'But life isn't fair it seems. You may not be my type, but you'll have to do.'

Audyn's mother's eyes widened. 'No!'

Gurm unhooked her and threw her on the ground.

'Don't look, Audyn! Don't look!' she screamed.

This time he listened to his mother. It was all his fault.

THE POWER OF PUNISHMENT

Audyn's mind felt like it was slipping away. If he wasn't looking at his mother and trying to see her as she was before they entered this shack of doom, he was staring at wooden planks. All day, every day - planks, his broken mother, three horrible men, his broken mother, more planks, no escape.

Footsteps approached again. The three monsters entered.

'Smells like a pig's muddy back-end in here,' Rowtes said, tossing his stone in the air and catching it.

Gurm threw a bucket of muddy water over Audyn's mother, while Nucri did the same to Audyn and gave him his daily kicking.

When Rowtes was done playing with his stone he hung Audyn's mother upside down from the beam again.

Nucri pointed a knife at Audyn while Gurm unchained him.

'Stand you little idiot,' Rowtes commanded.

Audyn stood and fell back against the wood. His legs creaked and his body ached.

'I'm bored of you both,' Rowtes said and turned to Audyn. 'So I need to make this more interesting. Every day, after I've had my fun with your mother, I'm going to hang her upside down for a while. In that time, we'll free you from your chains. When we return, if we see everything is normal, then this will remain your daily routine until one of you dies. Or, you could earn your freedom, by killing the hag.' Rowtes grinned and left the room.

His allies looked at each other. They didn't look as pleased with themselves as Rowtes did. They left.

'Kill me, Audyn. Please,' his mother begged.

'Never,' he said. His eyes filled with tears.

'It's the only way you can be free,' she said.

He stumbled over to her and hugged her. Even though she was upside down, just feeling her gave him hope.

Her grip tightened. 'Kill me! Kill me!'

He broke free and retreated to the wall.

'Please, Audyn! Please!'

He shook his head. 'It's not you I'm going to kill, Ma.'

The daily beatings continued and Audyn's heart ached every sunset. All he thought about was killing the men that made his mother's body crack. The men that twisted her arms, smacked her face and made her scream in that awful way.

He would kill them.

He sat, chained against the wall, and his mother stared at him.

'Do you want to hear a story?' she strained.

He shook his head.

'Do you want to hear a joke?' she asked.

He shook his head.

'What do you want to eat when we get out of here?' she asked.

He didn't respond. He couldn't even remember what his favourite food was. All he knew was that he hated potatoes.

'Please talk to me, my love,' she said.

He stared at her, that glimmer of hope still in her eyes.

She was an example of what happens when you are kind.

Kindness gets trampled on. It gets abused. The world is for those who take.

'I want to kill them all,' he said.

His mother shook her head. 'You promised me you would not become like them. Evil is a sickness, Audyn. It is something people pass on to each other with their actions, and you can either cure yourself of it by choosing a different action to them, or it will consume you and those around you. Don't become a spreader of evil.'

Audyn nodded. He heard the words, but they meant nothing. 'I'm not strong enough to be like you.'

'You are.' She shuffled against her chains. 'It's in your name. We named you after the Audyn herb, because it's used in helping people to recover from the most extreme sicknesses.'

He didn't care.

'I had a very difficult birth,' his mother said, 'and we thought you were going to die. The herb was our only hope but it grew so far away. You fought and fought, though. There were several nights I thought you were going to die. The colour faded from your skin and you cried and cried and coughed up everything you had inside of you. Every sunset the healer expected you to pass, but whenever you were in front of death you found something more. You refused to die. You gave your father the time he needed to find that herb. It was like you were powered by something else. Now, you need to use that strength to push these thoughts away.'

Audyn took a breath. That story meant nothing now. He wished he'd died as a baby, and if he was so strong why couldn't he break the chains? He stared at his mother and spoke with a calmness he hadn't felt before. 'I want to eat Rowtes' heart. I want to stab him in the legs, then stab him in the arms. I want it to be painful enough for him to scream, but I don't want him to die. I want to cut little pieces off him, one by one, sunset by sunset. And then I want to throw them on the floor next to him, so he can watch birds swoop down and peck at what was once a part of him. I want to see his tears. And I want to take that stone of his and ram it through his face.'

Audyn's mother stared at him. Through this entire ordeal her eyes held onto that faint hope. In that moment, it extinguished behind a flood of tears and her scream.

THE HARSHEST RELEASE

*A*udyn's mother struggled to look at him.

He hadn't spoken in a while, and it wasn't because he had stopped loving her. That would never happen. It was because any words that left his mouth were covered in such darkness they scared him as much as they scared her. Not because they were dark thoughts, but because he enjoyed them. They gave him energy, purpose.

The footsteps approached and the routine began. Washing, feeding, beating, grunting, then they hung Audyn's mother upside down. But before they left Audyn to consider killing her, Nucri put his healing tools down on a stool, ran out of the door and returned.

'Visitors. Quick!'

'Help!' Audyn's mother yelled.

'We're prisoners!' Audyn screamed. The darkness in his heart subsided and hope returned.

Rowtes whacked Audyn's mother and Gurm rushed to tie rope around her mouth and then Audyn's.

He screamed through the rope, but the sound barely reached

the end of the room. He moved his mouth, wriggled and writhed, desperate to squeeze a word out.

He stopped struggling and listened to the muffled conversation outside. He stared at his mother who stared back. They hung off every distorted word and sound.

Audyn's mother swung herself towards Nucri's tray. She jerked her head forward and knocked it off the stool. The implements crashed and rattled against the wood.

The muffled conversation became aggressive. Audyn was sure he heard a sword being unsheathed. A scream. A thud. Please…

Audyn's body tensed. Footsteps approached. Footsteps of freedom.

But the darkness spread over Audyn once more and his mother screamed into her rope.

Rowtes staggered in holding a bloody sword. Nucri and Gurm carried a soldier and dumped his stabbed body onto the wood.

Rowtes held his side where he had been slashed. He leaned on the sword. 'Got you both a friend.' He nodded to the body.

Nucri and Gurm untied the rope around Audyn's mother's mouth and released her arms.

They untied the rope silencing Audyn and unchained him.

'We'll be back in a while,' Rowtes said and they left.

Audyn and his mother cried in their unconventional hug.

'You know what you have to do, my love,' she told Audyn.

'I can't.'

She smiled at him. 'The thing is, my love, the worst thing you can do for me right now is to let me live.'

He hated that she was right. He was torturing her. He was no better than those men. 'I'll find a way to free us.' He had no idea how.

'Kill me and we're both free. Sometimes that's what love is. Helping people by doing something difficult.' She held his hands.

'Your father never left us. He was sick and dying, and in too much pain. He asked me to kill him.'

Audyn's first thought wasn't anger, but that she was making this up.

'I wanted to tell you, but he made me promise. He preferred that you thought he was bad instead of hating me for killing him. Even though I told him you would understand.'

Audyn stared at her. That numb feeling overcame him.

'Do you hate me, Audyn?' she asked.

'No. I hate the unfairness of the world.'

'Well, this is the last unfair thing you'll ever have to do,' she said. 'You can earn your freedom from unfairness.' She grabbed his hands. 'I'll put your hands where they need to be and you squeeze. After a few seconds, I'll be unconscious, but you have to keep squeezing. When my arms flop, squeeze for three hundred more seconds. It's how I had to do it with your father. But promise me, when you're free, don't stop being kind.'

He gave her one last kiss and through the coldness in his heart he managed to say, 'I love you.'

'I love you too.'

He nodded and she put his hands where they needed to go. He looked into her eyes and squeezed. Her neck moved under his thumbs. He desperately wanted to let go, but for her, living was torture.

Her grip on his hands loosened, her eyes widened and her hands fell from his to her sides. He couldn't look at her like this. He closed his eyes and counted, desperate to let go but he didn't want to let her down. He had to keep pressing, squeezing.

The flashes of them together flooded in. Building his room onto the shack. Story time under a full night sun. 'One hundred and ten.' Making all of their different shoes. 'One hundred and eighty-three.' Teaching him how to grow and dig up potatoes. But the smiles in all of those memories were gone. Now he kept seeing the faces of those three men. What if he was making a mistake? What if she wasn't thinking straight? 'Three hundred…'

He released her throat and stood there with his eyes closed. He didn't want to look at her so he turned around.

The footsteps approached, but he didn't care. The door opened.

'I can't believe you actually did it,' Rowtes said.

Audyn turned and saw the human waste holding a dagger.

'Shut up,' Audyn said.

Rowtes stepped towards Audyn and stabbed him in the stomach.

SECOND CHANCES

'He's awake! He's awake,' a woman's voice said.

'Ma?' Audyn asked. Every bone ached but he wasn't on the hard wood he had come to know. He was on a bed. Was it over? He tried to open his eyes but it was too bright. He squinted.

'Close the curtain, Leera,' the woman's voice said.

Audyn adjusted his eyes and a red-haired woman sat by him.

He screamed and swung his arms, but he was so frail she caught them. He had to escape.

'It's okay. You're okay.' She leaned over and held his arms against the bed.

He tried to fight but his arms felt as if they could tear.

'You're safe. I won't hurt you,' the woman said.

He focused his eyes on her slender face. He would think it was a kind face, but he didn't know the difference between kind and awful anymore.

'Have some water.' She held a tankard.

He nodded and a part of him feared she would whack the tankard against his head.

The woman got up and Audyn noticed her wooden leg. She helped him to sit up and poured the water into his mouth. It was incredible to taste water without mud in it. He felt it flow through his body and hoped it wasn't poisoned.

A brown-haired girl, about his own age, stood behind the woman.

The woman sat back down. 'I'm Thana, and this is my girl, Leera.' She put an arm around her daughter and stared at Audyn. 'You are?'

The thought of his name hurt. He didn't want anyone to know it. It was the name of the boy who killed his mother. It was the boy who was weak. He shook his head.

'Very well. I'll call you Boy. That okay?'

He nodded.

'Leera, get our guest some more water, please.'

Leera took the tankard from Audyn and left the bedroom.

Thana leaned in. 'Boy. I've never seen someone survive wounds like yours and I was in two wars.'

Audyn looked at his body. Stab wounds covered his torso and legs. Skin stretched around cuts, and bruises made his body look like an ugly painting, He recoiled at himself. He remembered none of it after the first stab.

'You can stay here as long as you need, but if when you're better you're still here, I'll have to put you to work.'

He nodded.

'How old are you?' Thana asked.

He shook his head. 'I was seven the last time I had any sense of the sunsets. I don't know any more.'

Audyn spent over forty sunsets recovering and regaining the feeling of movement without agony.

He hated sleeping. Whenever he went to sleep his mother haunted his dreams. The hitting, the grunting, the begging. He would wake up sweating and crying, then he couldn't get back to bed. He'd lay there replaying his ordeal in the shack.

Thana helped him to rebuild some of his strength with balancing tasks and tests.

They were the most frustrating sunsets of his life, but every time he progressed is was like he was coming alive again.

His least favourite test was the fence run. He had to sprint to the fence across the field then back before a leaky bucket ran out of water. He always failed, either falling or running out of breath. He didn't know why, but as the tiredness kicked in and the thoughts of failing the task crept up on him, so would images of the shack and his torture. Thana remained emotionless when he would eventually fall to the ground and gasp for air. She'd walk away. 'Again at first light tomorrow,' she'd say. She told him the best work was done at first light, before the nonsense of the world began.

Thana kept him well fed and never let him slack. No matter how much he groaned, threw up, or cried.

There were times he hated her for it, but she wasn't hurting him, and he noticed progress. His muscles were growing.

He'd get closer and closer to conquering the fence run, until finally, one day he made it.

Thana actually smiled and Leera clapped.

As soon as Audyn was healthy enough to walk he considered leaving, but where would he go? He still couldn't fend for himself in a world of unknowns.

He approached Thana as she lay in the field reading to Leera. Thana lived in the middle of nothingness, but it was calming. He liked that he could see all around, so he could prepare himself if anyone approached.

'Thana.'

'Yes, Boy.' She sat up and pulled blades of grass up.

He clasped his hands together. 'I want to stay and work.'

Thana nodded. 'Okay.' She looked at Leera who nodded too and smiled.

'But I also want you to train me. Like when you were a soldier. I want to be strong.'

Thana's mouth curled into a smile.

PERMANENCE

*A*udyn wanted to get strong enough to fight anyone who ever tried to attack him, but also because training distracted him. He could focus his anger, his fear, and see the results of it. His body needed it more than food.

He grew rapidly. The training built muscles on muscles and he loved to admire himself in the water's reflection when he would wash.

They would train for hours in the morning, in the open field under the sunrise, in the snow, even when the rain hammered their faces and they slipped in the mud. The only conversation would be Thana teaching him proper techniques. Then in the evenings they would eat and stretch, which brought back memories of potato picking with his mother. It made him sad but reminded him that they had memories not involving torture. After stretching, Thana, and sometimes Audyn, would read Leera stories.

Audyn learned how to use a sword, axe, bow and arrow, but his favourite training was with his fists. Thana told him to never underestimate the value of your fists in a sword fight. 'Often people are too busy swinging their steel to use the most flexible weapons they have.'

Every training session would end with combat, and every day he lost. He was always thinking of the people who ruined his life as he fought - Gurm, Rowtes, Nucri, Sabata, Uldeen, Agra.

Their faces would haunt him and break his focus and that was all Thana needed. Even when he tried to shut them out, his mother's image would flash in his mind, but not a happy memory. She'd be hanging upside down.

Every day he tried, and every day he failed. He tried striking Thana's wooden leg, but it may as well have been a normal one.

She always had advice. 'What you see as someone's greatest weakness, they may have turned into their biggest strength, and what you see as their most dominant feature could be their undoing,' she would say. He had no idea what her dominant feature was, though. All of her was dominant.

It got to the point where he would train alone when she was done. He had to beat her, and he believed that if he kept training he would. But he was wrong.

He asked her why. Why couldn't he beat her, even with all that practice?

'Because I'm stronger and I trained that strength to the point where I will always be ahead of you. The only way you'll beat me is if I stop training, and that will never happen.'

He couldn't accept it. He practiced more. Before the sun rose, with her, then when it went down again, without her. A year went by with extra sessions. He found himself thinking of his mother less and less every day, and he hated himself for it. The night hauntings got worse though, like she was trying to cling on to him.

Today was the day he would beat Thana. He was sure of it. They trained and then prepared for battle. Today it was swords.

He took the first swing and she blocked, but stumbled slightly and smiled. They clashed swords and he punched her in the ribs.

'Good,' she said.

Their swords clashed again and he went for the same punch but she caught his fist and kicked the side of his knee. He buckled.

She pushed his sword away from hers, struck her sword handle between his neck and shoulder, then held her sword to his face. 'Halt.'

He bowed his head.

'Nearly, Boy. Nearly,' she said.

He looked at the mud. *Rowtes, Sabata, Nucri, Gurm, Agra, Uldeen.*

He roared and lunged, but she blocked.

'Boy?'

He swung down and she blocked.

'Halt! Halt Boy!'

Nucri, Gurm, Sabata, Agra, Rowtes, Uldeen.

He swung again. And again. And again. She slipped further back.

'I said halt!'

He swung again and again. Bash, bash, bash until the pressure cracked her wooden leg and she buckled. He swung his sword and stopped it an inch from her face.

She stared up at him and he burst into tears, dropped the sword and fell to his knees. 'I'm sorry!'

CHANCE OF A LIFETIME

The kitchen was silent. He slurped his soup off the spoon and struggled to look up at Thana. He had apologised and apologised and she said it was fine, but it wasn't fine. He wasn't fine.

He finally looked up from his bowl to find her staring at him.

'Boy, I think it's time I gave you a choice.' She placed her spoon on the wooden table.

He didn't like choices. He remembered the choice Rowtes had given him.

'That look I see in your eyes every day. I don't like it, but I understand it. I saw it just after a war, and I used to wear that look. Only reason I washed it off my face was because of her.' She nodded at Leera.

'So, I can find peace?' he asked.

'That's up to you. You can stay here, become part of my family and lead a normal life. I'll find you work at a market in Lansort. Or, you can go and do whatever it is you've been training so hard to go and do.' She raised her finger. 'But. If you go, you *never* come back here. I don't want trouble blowing through that door, so if I see you on the horizon I'll put an arrow through your face.'

She took a breath and picked up her spoon. 'Think about it tonight and tell me tomorrow.' She took another mouthful of soup.

He stared at her a moment. She had made him feel safe again. It was because of her kindness. But, what happened today wasn't something he could control. How could he ever be truly safe when he was the danger? Safety was temporary while the memories that haunted him were permanent. They would only die with him. Tomorrow could be peaceful, but the following day could be hellish.

He didn't need to wait until the morning. He stood up and walked around the table. He extended his hand to Thana who stood up and hugged him, but what should have been a warm moment felt cold.

'I understand. Thank you for letting me train you,' Thana said.

Audyn looked at Leera who smiled as tears formed in her eyes.

The names wrecked his mind again.

Sabata, Uldeen, Rowtes, Gurm, Agra, Nucri.

But he would no longer let them be a poison. They would become his motivation.

Rowtes, Agra, Gurm, Nucri, Uldeen, Sabata.

Rowtes.

Agra.

Gurm.

Nucri.

Uldeen.

Sabata.

He pulled away from the hug. 'My name is Ragnus.' The only thing he could control was his strength, and he would set about becoming as strong as Thana, if not stronger. Somewhere in the world, there would be a way.

RAGNUS

Ragnus tried to sleep in the back of the carriage, partly to pass the time, but mostly to shut out the ramblings of the two old men opposite him. But he jolted awake whenever the carriage would roll over a stone or an uneven piece of ground. He wondered if he would ever sleep properly again. It was as though his mind was always alert, waiting to fight back.

The men spoke about what they would do with their new homes, how many wives they would have, and how much ale they would drink.

'What will you do when we arrive?' the one with the red rash around his mouth asked Ragnus.

Ragnus looked out of the window at the plains. 'I'll see where the mood takes me.'

The men chuckled. The one with the rash turned to the one with three teeth. 'Clearly still a virgin.' They laughed louder than was necessary.

The night sun rose and Ragnus recognised the landscape. His heart hardened.

'Do you mind if we stop for a toilet break?' Ragnus asked. 'I know somewhere.'

Ragnus' breath quickened as they neared. He thought he would be ready, but when the carriage stopped he had to take deep breaths. He remembered Thana's technique, so held his breath and stared at one point until things calmed.

He gazed out of the carriage window. Rowtes sat in front a fire with his back to the carriage.

'Isn't he going to greet us?' the three-toothed man said.

The one with the red rash opened the door and shouted, 'Any chance of a quick wee?'

Rowtes didn't turn around. He pointed to his left. 'That shack, there.'

'Quite the charmer,' the three-toothed man said.

The old men climbed out of the carriage and went to the toilet.

Ragnus stepped out of the carriage and stared at the back of Rowtes' head. He wanted to crush it.

He walked to his old shack. It was exactly as he'd left it, only now a home to the spider-worms and their webs. He poked his head into his mother's room. Her clothes were still there and all the different pairs of boots. He had a selection of her memories at his disposal.

He picked up the pitchfork and left the shack.

He walked towards Rowtes who stared at the grass, his sharp stone in his hands. Ragnus stood in front of him.

Rowtes' face was covered in hair and lines of age and misery.

Ragnus dug the pitchfork into the soil to get Rowtes' attention.

Rowtes gazed up at him, nodded and said in a defeated tone. 'I don't care anymore.'

Ragnus expected more.

The old men returned to the carriage. 'Young fellow, are you ready?'

He raised a hand for them to wait.

'Rude,' one of them said.

Rowtes spat on the mud. 'I'm sorry. I know what I did was wrong, and it's haunted me every day that I've sat in this hell.'

Ragnus noticed two graves in distance. 'I suppose the respectful burials are for your friends and not my mother?'

Rowtes nodded. 'We burned her. You can do whatever you want to me. I deserve it.'

Pathetic.

Ragnus lifted the pitchfork out of the soil and jammed it into Rowtes' thigh. He yelped and fell off his stool and onto the soil.

'What are you doing?' the man with the red rash yelled.

'Wait in the carriage!' Ragnus said.

The two men hastily entered the carriage.

Ragnus placed his boot on Rowtes' thigh and yanked the pitchfork out. Rowtes wept.

Ragnus wanted to do what he had told his mother. He wanted to eat his heart, to cut him into pieces. But looking at Rowtes, he deserved something more appropriate.

He stepped on Rowtes' hand and took the stone, placing it in his pocket. He dragged Rowtes by the legs and took him into the shack where he and his mother had been imprisoned and tortured.

Ragnus threw Rowtes against the wall and he slumped against it.

Ragnus took the sharp stone from his pocket and squeezed the back of Rowtes' head. He pressed the stone into Rowtes' mouth, but his teeth seemed to be in the way.

Ragnus pushed the stone hard. The grinding sound filled his soul with relief.

Rowtes screamed into the stone and saliva spilled out of the small gaps between it and the corners of his mouth.

'You should have stabbed me a few more times.' Ragnus pushed the stone harder. Rowtes' teeth cracked and his saliva ran red with blood.

Ragnus dragged Rowtes away from the wall so he was lying down.

Rowtes stared up at Ragnus, full of fear, the stone half wedged into his mouth and his eyes red and bulging.

Ragnus stomped the stone through his face.

Rowtes' body went limp and Ragnus felt nothing.

Absolutely nothing.

His breathing was as calm as though he had just been for a stroll.

Ragnus left the room, lit a torch from the fire and set every building in Gemeria alight, his mother's belongings too. He rejoined the old men in the carriage.

They didn't say a word for the rest of the trip to Romoro and exchanged the odd concerned glance with each other.

As the journey continued, Ragnus felt numb. What was next? He wondered if he should have stayed with Thana, but then he smiled to himself. He was powerful and still so young. However, Thana had shown him that no matter what, there would always be someone stronger out there. If that person decided they wanted to ruin Ragnus' life, then what could he do?

He would become the strongest being in Hastovia, so that he never had to feel inferior to anyone again.

The End

ACKNOWLEDGMENTS

Thank you to anyone who feels like they need to be thanked. You deserve it. Thank you with all of the thanks in Thanksland

THANK YOU

Thank you for reading!

Karl's Kingdom Book 3: In Memory Of... Will be available in 2020 and you can find more info at www.mark-boutros.com

If you haven't joined my mailing list, you can at www.mark-boutros.com/crew
You'll get exclusive offers and stuff you probably don't want or need

If you enjoyed the book, please leave a review, and once again thank you for reading